WHITE MAN'S PROBLEMS

WHITE MAN'S PROBLEMS

STORIES BY KEVIN MORRIS

Black Cat
New York

Originally published in 2014 by Sweet Devil Press,
Los Angeles, CA

Printed in the United States of America

ISBN 978-0-8021-2388-6
eISBN 978-0-8021-9142-7

Black Cat
a paperback original imprint of Grove/Atlantic, Inc.
154 West 14th Street
New York, NY 10011

Distributed by Publishers Group West

www.groveatlantic.com

15 16 17 18   10 9 8 7 6 5 4 3 2 1

For my mom, Betsy

"After a certain age every man is responsible for his own face."
-Albert Camus

"There is nothing to do but go home and drink your nine drinks and forget about it."
-Donald Barthelme

Contents

WHITE MAN'S PROBLEMS

Summer Farmer

When Harrigan awoke, the first thing he saw was her left eye with its cobalt-blue iris. She'd snuck into his bed again. He didn't mind it. Any single dad is happy when his nine-year-old daughter gets in bed with him. Beautiful, really, that eye—those eyes. Ruby was tugging his arm, telling him to get up. It was early, and he knew she wanted to watch TV for those few valuable minutes before her nanny made it through the surfer traffic of the Pacific Coast Highway to the house on Malibu Road.

He turned on the cartoons and walked to the medicine cabinet, where he swallowed his morning meds. There were six pills: three Lamictal and three Budeprion XL, the generic brand of Wellbutrin. They picked him up and slowed him down—at least that's how the psychopharmacologist explained it. He was a touch bipolar; how big the touch and how far apart the poles, no one knew. He thought the pills helped, but there was evidence they didn't.

He made his daily fiber-supplement drink and waited for a cappuccino to drip from the machine. One of the artificially distressed kitchen cabinets was losing a handle, another thing to fix. The beach and the sky and the ocean were gray. He read the *New York Times* more closely than the *LA Times*, and didn't read the *Wall Street Journal* at all. He shifted from left to right, making room for Ruby's brother, Bobby, as he sat sleepy eyed and grouchy, an unspeaking beast, all zits and hair in a Dead Kennedys T-shirt.

Once the nanny arrived, he backed out of the garage and headed slowly south along the shoreline in his black Mercedes S 63 AMG. It had a 518-horsepower V-8 AMG engine, F1 manual shifters, twenty-inch five-spoke light alloy wheels, seven-speed automatic transmission, and calibrated Active Body Control. The S 63 also had AMG-specific piping design and new contoured side bolsters for outstanding seating comfort, as well as an MSRP of $127,000. He wasn't sure what he paid; his business manager had handled it.

The feeling of wealth was still odd for him, so far away from his start. When the doctors had asked for family history, he traced his genealogy to the potato famine of 1845. His eight great-great-grandfathers, to a man, were listed in church records as "gravediggers." Descendants who made it to Baltimore, while they managed to find work out of ditches, did not prosper in the New World. He often wondered how, over the course of 150 years in America, such a big family could not manage to scrape together a goddamn dime.

He pulled into the Starbucks at Cross Creek. There was the usual line of people: moms who just dropped the kids at school, contractors dicking around, evangelical Pepperdine kids. The barista had a nose ring and caramel hair streaked with orange. The women stole glances at him. He spoke to no one, avoiding eye contact by staring at the kids' menu. Chocolate-chip Frappuccinos and Rice Krispies treats. He hated the way they announced the drinks. "Grande vanilla latte for Dennis." Humiliating.

He went stop-and-go down the coast until he hit a lineup at Topanga. He did not put the headset on; he did not roll calls. He moved in traffic amid no sounds at all: no radio, no CDs, no iPhone. He rode in silence as often as he could lately. He even stopped listening to the Dodgers, who were hopeless. The phone rang. His assistant told him she had Stern, his regular psychologist. Harrigan said he'd call back. What could Stern tell him? What would he ask? "Are you still crazy?"

He drove south past the Santa Monica beaches and the volleyball courts and the eroding cliffs of Palisades Park. Past the pier and through the McClure Tunnel where the PCH becomes the I-10 and the sign read *Christopher Columbus Transcontinental Highway*. He asked himself, his ritual, "What if I just keep driving?" How far he could go, how long he would last with the assumed names, the hotel rooms, the paying in cash, he did not know. He felt gravity was sideways, that he should be further east, that he was of the Atlantic. He missed the changing seasons and the touch of holy water in the foyer; he missed the cold, dark, freezing rain.

But the western-most point of the eastbound I-10 was where he was in his life. He had long ago become rich producing movies, a vocation that suited him well. There was a house on the beach, a house in the mountains, stock positions, bond ladders, hedge funds for growth, hedge funds for value, and hedge funds for hedging against hedge funds. He let three-hundred-dollar gift certificates expire under other papers stuffed in his desk. Wealth insulated him from the grinding existence of his parents and siblings. But nothing prepared him for what had happened and the pain that visited his soul. The engine of his sleek, black, luxury car was overheating, drying up all its fluids. Harrigan was not young or old. The world had flattened and he'd become a cliché headed east.

How predictable and boring it was to be depressed. He'd heard about it, read about it, been warned about it, and now, right on schedule, he was living it. The source of the depression was no mystery, oldest one in the books. But as he made the drive each day, talked on the phone, had lunch, finished up work at the office, looked at Bobby's homework, and did all the other things that made up his life, he knew it was not what had happened. It was that he was not better, that he couldn't do better, and that he had broken his word.

He turned onto Avenue of the Stars. Century City was 20.7 miles from his home on the Pacific in Malibu. A dozen or so high rises, two large modern shopping centers, and a couple hotels. It was past Westwood and before Beverly Hills, between the country club for WASPs and the country club for Jews. He played golf at both but was a member of neither. Century City: a monstrosity of the modern, bastard child of the scumbags of real estate and the whores of show business. There was nothing in the name — Century City — that justified the importance, the primacy, the notion that it was at the center of things. It was in the center of nothing. Like everything in LA, it was an illusion.

He pulled into his building, past the guards and through the automatic card reader and into the lower circles of the parking lot. His reserved spot was next to the service elevator, which was an express to his floor, saving a trip through the lobby. A small man in blue coveralls was already waiting, which was not unusual. Taking the service entrance meant that Harrigan often rode with the working guys, the electricians, caulkers, framers, and the like. Seeing them made him think of his dad and his uncles, who carried pressure gauges and tape measures and had specks of drywall in the hairs of their forearms at the end of the day. They were far away from him now.

———

The little man smiled at him. There was a big *O* above his pocket, the insignia of the Otis Elevator Company. His nametag said *Kingsley*, which was a bit confusing to Harrigan, because the guy appeared to be Mexican—a little light skinned but definitely Mexican. He wore a small gold bracelet with a young girl's face, a photo image engraved on a charm.

Harrigan felt a stir. "Is that your daughter?" he asked.

Kingsley looked at his bracelet and held it up. "Yes."

The elevator didn't seem to be moving, so Kingsley stepped up and pressed the button, as though he were responsible for the delay. He stepped back and stared ahead.

"She died."

"Oh, good lord," Harrigan said. "I'm so sorry." Then, after a second, he asked, "How old was she?"

"She was nine. Car accident."

Harrigan usually let this type of moment pass. But after the car came and the two men got on, he spoke up. "I lost mine, too," he said. "A daughter...my daughter."

"Aah. I'm sorry. How old?"

"Seven. Eighteen months ago." He poked at the button for his floor. "Leukemia."

"Then you know all about it, my friend."

"Yes, I do. I'm afraid I do."

It is true of any of us that, should a stranger meet us at the intersection of elevator and automobile when the chill cloud of memory hits; if he should recognize the subterranean cascade of longing and remorse; if he knows well the depthless sadness of not seeing a child rise into the brace-face, the inappropriate midriff, the biology major, the bride; he would be privy not just to the naked basis of our being but to our utter defenselessness to the lateral and vertical rhythms and movement of this world.

———

Kingsley dropped off his paperwork at the management office and rode the elevator back down to his truck. He had received the call after midnight to service the broken car for floors eleven through twenty. As he went through the payment kiosk, he teased the Ethiopian girl who took his money, telling her he was coming back to take her away with him. She tried not to, but she laughed, only the latest to learn there was no resisting Manuel Kingsley.

He pulled onto Century Park West heading east, thinking about how beautiful the buildings were. Architecture, to him, was man's way of talking to heaven. He enjoyed getting called to Century City, because it made him feel special. It was fancier than downtown or the Valley, where his work usually was. It was closer to the heart of show business, and Kingsley, like so many, was a sucker for the excitement of Hollywood. He could feel that in the buildings. And, man, those buildings, they were a wonder.

As he drove down Olympic, he saw he was low on gas: the digital monitor told him he had sixty miles before empty. Enough to get home to his wife so she wouldn't worry. He could fill up later. He turned on the wipers, and the cleaning fluid washed the dust away. Kingsley felt lucky to see the marvel in things. After Opal died, eleven years ago, he vowed not to waste his spirit. And he had kept this vow, for the most part, aided by the knowledge there were lots of people who didn't have it too good. He had known great sadness, but it had not claimed him. He thought of this as Opal's gift.

Nor had money possessed him. It lost its hold when she died. Gradually, his taste for life came back, but finances would never again keep him up at night. He wished for things, sure. He wanted more time. He had fantasies about young girls. His back hurt in the morning. But he got what he needed, some fishing in San Pedro and an old man's love of golf. And family and friends, all healthy, thank God.

At sixty-two, Kingsley did not feel alienated from anything. He wasn't going from left to right or right to left. Life was like an elevator ride: ups and downs. He helped people get up in the morning and go home to their families at night. He took pride in the efficient delivery of millions to places all over the city. These were not coping mechanisms, but the abiding convictions of faith, for Manuel Kingsley was not a man whose mind defaulted to worries about work.

He made the transition from the Santa Monica Freeway in the west to the Pasadena Freeway headed east. He switched on the radio and a guitar solo blared, reminding him of Casey. Kingsley laughed thinking how much his life had come to revolve around a twelve-year-old named Casey Evans. Opal's sister, Ophelia, had married Scott Evans, a quiet guy who worked with computers. Kingsley's wife had been against the white boy at first, but after all they'd been through, Kingsley told Ophelia to follow her heart. He could not refuse her anything. And Scott had won him over by learning all about elevators, the subject that Kingsley loved better than best.

He parked the truck on the Doran side of the Starbucks on Glendale Avenue, deciding to stop even though he was on the flip side of his usual morning. No one in Starbucks ever really knew if he had just worked all night or was setting off for the day. He craved the caramel Frappuccinos and snuck one in every morning. He knew all the workers and ordered the usual from the kid at the register. They talked about the Angels, who were always in it these days. He saw Barbara behind the counter. He asked for a report on her son, a linebacker at Crenshaw. As they chatted, she gave him his drink, and he pushed it back with a frown. She said, "Manny, you know you ain't supposed to have it." Then she relented and gave him a little shot of whipped cream, their private joke once more made.

As he headed back out on Glendale Avenue, his mind traveled again. He thought about his grandfather, long-dead white man in Mexico, eccentric vagabond from England, reader of Shakespeare. He thought of his mother, who lived with his sister and her family in Uvalde. They had all come to Los Angeles in the fifties and lived off Olvera Street, working in the shops and washing dishes. So much had happened in fifty years, so much was left behind, and so much was gone. Yet memory did not diminish the charge he felt driving alone in his truck, headed east to a home that he owned in California. In America.

He owed it all to elevators. Twenty-six years in a business that set him free. Kingsley was trained to repair the Gearless Traction Model, the workhorse of the industry and the predominant machine in LA. The GTE could go five hundred feet per minute, with steel cables attached to the top of the car and wrapped around the drive sheave in special grooves. The transfer between the weight of the car and the counterweight attached by cables moved the machine. Ninety-five percent of all problems were caused by faulty upkeep or someone pushing the wrong buttons. There was a confession in almost every call for repair.

He parked in the driveway of his house and looked at the digital readout from the gas gauge: thirty-nine miles till empty. The sprinklers for the front flowerbed were on and Manny's work shoes got wet. A warm, brown light followed him when he opened the door. His wife was already cleaning the house. She smiled and went into the kitchen. He sat down at the Formica table and looked at the papers, *La Opinión* and the *LA Times*. She put out plates of scrambled eggs and tortillas, popping up and down to get what she thought he needed. She made him eat the bran muffin he hated.

They spoke Spanish in the quiet voices of old friends. He was tired, yes, but he would be ok later. He moved into the living room and put on ESPN with the sound down low. She closed the old gold curtains so the room would be cool and he would have shade for his nap. She brought a glass of water and a handful of pills: Lipitor, Atenolol, Myleran, vitamins, and antioxidants. The Myleran, a large oval pill, made him nauseous. But he was only on it for six more weeks, when there would be another scan.

As he settled into in the soft, deep, red quiet, he glanced at the photos near his head, on the table at the end of the couch where he lay. The old black-and-whites of his parents in Mexico were crowded out by a group picture of the Kingsleys and Evanses at the wedding. There were lots of sports action shots and team plaques off to the side and a very special Polaroid of Casey and Manny on the golf course at Arroyo Seco. Manny kept looking, though, and found the one he was after this morning. It was Opal when she was a toddler in his arms at the beach. She was looking at the camera from over his shoulder. Manny's back was turned, but his profiled face smiled up at her. He looked at his little girl closely now, as he had done a million times before, paying particular attention to those big, beautiful, brown, and round eyes.

The Plot To Hold Hands
With Elizabeth Tremblay

It is not cool that people around here think it's ok. It's bad enough that grown men are going to beauty salons, sitting under hair dryers, walking around like poodles, and saying "Do you like my perm?" Bad enough that we have pet rocks and mood rings. But if that isn't enough for you, if that doesn't show the ridiculous state of affairs here in late-seventies America, consider this: we have to live with the knowledge that someone, somewhere, thinks it is ok for the Philadelphia Phillies' away uniforms to be baby blue. They wear goddamn baby blue uniforms on the road. Am I the only one who is ashamed? And while we're on the subject, they screwed up the P in Phillies, making it round and puffy and completely stupid looking. The kind of P the Pillsbury Doughboy would pick if he was running the club.

I am sitting in detention. My first one. Two hours of forced confinement after school. It's jail-like. Actually, there are many similarities between my school and a penitentiary. We went on a field trip to the state prison at Graterford a few months ago—which is pretty bizarre when you think about it, but that's another whole road—and the thing I remember most is that it kind of looked like our high school. Both are made of reddish brick, concrete, and feature wonderful painted-cinder-block interiors. Both have lots of gray railings and windows with chain linking inside the glass. I don't know how they do that with the windows.

My English teacher, Mr. Matthews, must get an extra twenty bucks to sit through this, which he probably needs if you go by the way he scrunches his face as he balances his checkbook. He sees me come in today and says, "Budding, what are you doing here?"

I don't want to get into the whole thing, so I say, "I got into trouble. It's a long story."

He gives me a distrustful look. "Ok, I'll find out what you did. But you're going to have to work while you're here." He gestures at the other fifteen detainees in the room. "You don't get to just sit around like those other morons."

I look around for some help, but seeing the scuzzballs in detention with me, I realize Mr. Matthews kind of has a point.

He thinks about it. "I want you to get something out of this," he says. "Otherwise it's no punishment. Write something. I won't read it."

Let me go through my day. At 6:32 a.m., the clock radio goes off in the bedroom I share with my little brother. It's the same freaking jingle every morning: "Another great day is with us, and to start it out happi-ly, we'd like to be the first to *say good morning and to welcome you to W-I-P...in Phil-a-del-phia...*" My mother calls me just as I fall back to sleep. "Ro-man!" It's about fifteen degrees outside. I know this because my dad accidentally shut the door of our room after we went to bed, so no heat came in all night, which means the day starts with us seeing our breath. I take my school clothes into the bathroom because I will get frostbite if I walk back to my bedroom in a towel.

My mom is so bleary she can't make breakfast. Nobody wants to eat anyway, because it's so frickin' cold and early. I toast one piece of Wonder Bread and go to the bus stop with my little brother, Bill. I'd like to point out here that he gets named "Bill" and I get named "Roman." That gives you an idea of my parents. We live in a place called Stuckley, named after a guy who, best I can tell, is famous for owning a farm. At the bus stop, my hair is frozen under my hat and, once again, I am freezing my ass off. I look down the street for any sign of yellow. Bill and I huddle with the other kids like a stranded bobsled team waiting for the rescue vehicle.

We get on the bus, and Anthony, the driver, gives me five bucks. The guy always takes the Eagles, which is really not smart. We are on the bus from 7:10 till 7:40. The heaters blow like crazy, and it gets hotter as the bus collects kids. Since I'm wearing a big jacket over two shirts and a sweater, I start to sweat. And as I heat up, I start to fall asleep again. It's like being tortured. The only thing that pulls me out of it is that Elizabeth Tremblay gets on when we get to Riddlewood, where the nice houses are. She sits two rows in front of me. She is the hottest girl in the school and I am in love with her. I give her a little wave when she walks near me, and she says hi. She sits with her friend Jane Ragni, who is a cheerleader, too. I usually try to say something funny, but there is no opening today.

Ok, maybe everybody else thinks Jane is the hottest girl in the school. Not me. For me it's Liz; she's my dream girl. She has brown hair, green eyes, the right kind of freckles, and a beautiful, if a little bit round, face. She's got a nice body with good boobs. But the thing about Liz is her butt. It's the best in the world. She doesn't have a little bony behind like Jane's. Liz' is a nice round thing. It looks like two horseshoes side-by-side.

Or, to put it another way, imagine the letter W. Most girls in ninth grade have butts in which the middle part of the W is made up of straight, angular lines. Not Liz Tremblay. With her, the W is made with big curvy lines, like the W for Wilson Baseball gloves. Or the W the Pillsbury Doughboy would make if he was making a W — which would be a better use of the Pillsbury Doughboy's time, by the way, than making baseball uniforms.

After we herd off the bus, I have ten minutes to drop my books off at my locker and get to my first class, which, of course, is gym. Next thing I know, I'm putting on my uniform, which I always forget to take home. It's so not clean. It has a little bit of an ammonia smell. Jock strap, shorts, and shirt. For some reason, the phys ed teacher, Mr. Lambert, is obsessed with wrestling. I swear to God we've been wrestling for eight months. Every Monday, Wednesday, and Friday at 8:00 a.m. I can be found wrestling Peter Logatelli. Now, I like Peter. Nothing against him. But he weighs 280 pounds. I mean, Jesus Christ, they're going to cut him out of a house someday. And they don't give us any kneepads or anything.

Today I am getting smushed as usual by the tubolard Logatelli when Lambert comes by. "Sit-out, Budding. Perfect time for a sit-out!" When I try to sit-out, which is just a dumbass wrestling coach way of saying "get the hell away from the guy," I go nowhere. My legs just flail around under Peter's sumo-like mass. My knees and shins make a skidding noise as they get burned on the mat. I'm leaving skin behind like a molting snake.

The other annoying thing about gym class is you have to take a shower when it's over. So, about ten minutes before the bell, it's off we go from the mat to the locker room. I strip down naked and take my towel to the shower. A couple of points here: First, I always forget to take my towel home, too. It's gray—at least now it's gray—and it's about as big as a standard washcloth. It doesn't cover me at all. Not fun. Second, it's ice cold in the locker room because some idiot left the door to the football field open. It's a goddamn pattern. It's back to freezing my gonads off until I go into the shower, which is about eight thousand degrees and ignites the burns on my legs. Then they make you step on an athlete's-foot machine, which is basically two metal pedals that squirt disinfectant onto your feet. I am grateful for the school's interest in my hygiene—I really am—but I don't think that thing works.

The forced march continues as I go to geometry, which starts at 8:49. (Every minute counts with the assholes who make up this schedule.) I have to sprint to make it, causing perspiration again. But once I get there, I realize I don't have anything to do, because I finished the problems last week. There's a rumor that today we will dissect frogs in sixth-period biology. You have to understand that this is a very big deal for the ninth grade. We've never done anything like that before. The girls are all scared shitless.

My geometry teacher is Mr. Lutz, an old crabby guy. The kids hate him. Today, five minutes into the lesson, he gets mad at a football player, Jeff Zwarts, for talking. He sends him to the blackboard and proceeds to give him the business. He says, "Draw a quadrangle." Zwarts does it. "Ok, Mr. Zwarts, that is your head. You are a blockhead." Laughter erupts. Then Lutz says, "Now, Mr. Zwarts, please make the best possible circle you can." Zwarts makes a pretty decent circle. "Draw the radius of the circle." Zwarts has no clue. Lutz looks at me. Just as I was afraid of, he says, "Mr. Budding, draw the radius." So I make a face that says *don't kill me* to Zwarts as I go up to the board and make a line from the outer edge of the circle to the middle. Lutz says, "Zwarts, put your nose on the point at the end of the radius going away from the circumference, which is the diametric center point of the circle." Zwarts sticks his nose against the board, and now his back is to the rest of the class. "Ok, Mr. Zwarts, we will get back to you." He leaves Zwarts there till the bell thirty-eight minutes later — 9:44.

Third period is music, which starts at 9:52. The teacher is Mrs. Weaver, who is a hippy with hippyish body odor. I don't know what's so musical about her. It's like all hippies are assumed to be musical. Anyway, she has us playing recorder, which is basically a plastic tube with holes. At the beginning of class, she sends us to the front of the room to pick an instrument out of the laundry bin. The school that is so worried about my athlete's foot apparently does not care about the canker sores I will get from a recorder used by six other students per day. Disgusting. But that's nothing compared to what happens when thirty-five ninth graders start trying to play "The Entertainer."

See, the thing about recorders is that after you blow on them awhile, saliva starts coming out the bottom. I'm standing next to Ernie Bundt, with whom I am going through life for the sole reason that our names fall next to each other alphabetically. No one can produce more slobber than Ernie. There's the fountain of youth, there are fountains of knowledge, and then there's Ernie Bundt, a fountain of drool. The worst part is Liz Tremblay is sitting right behind me. If you have a crush on someone, slobbering out of your recorder is the kind of thing you try to avoid. I accomplish this by going into a lot of stylish flourishes. I raise my horn horizontally like I'm Wynton Marsalis every time I think spit is coming out. That's kind of gross, though, because if I go too high the drool comes back into my mouth from the other direction.

Speaking of Liz, she's smart — maybe the smartest cheerleader in the history of the school. She speaks French and knows about art and all. We're in the "Academically Talented" classes together, which seems a little brutal on the other kids. My friend Hubie is in the C section. My dad says you might as well say "fill it up" when you put a kid in the C section. My mom smacks dad when he talks like that.

Anyway, the classes thing gives me a lot of playing time with Liz. The problem is she hangs with the cool people, the kids in the normal classes, like the A and B sections, which are made up of her cheerleader friends and the jocks and the whole road that goes down. In other words, she's in with the normal people. I don't have the same kind of hookup. My cred is very high with the smart crowd, but when it comes to the cool kids, it's like you have to hide that you're intelligent. It's a dilemma.

She sits next to me in seventh-period study hall. This gives me the opportunity to wear her down with conversation and jokes. We've actually started having real long talks. I try to read up on things that will interest her, like witchcraft and the Rosenbergs. I even watch what I wear, which is tough. To tell the truth, sometimes I worry she won't stoop down to going out with me because it would be socially unacceptable. Other times I think, what the hell? I'm a pretty cool guy. She should go out with me. I get jealous thinking about her with anyone else. Man, I don't like the way that feels. It gets me way down deep, like in some molten center of my body, like the ball of fire in the middle of the earth. Sometimes I wake up at night wondering if that ball is going to burn through me and once it's done turn into a huge, exploding fire that destroys the world. I'm a little nuts like that.

Music ends at 10:47, and we head to the cafeteria for lunch. We push the orange trays along the aluminum railing, and from behind the Plexiglas barrier they serve us spaghetti with meat sauce. Dessert, their apology for the entrée, is a little square of red Jell-O with some half-assed whipped cream on top. At this point, I'm not that into eating anything, let alone this shit. It isn't yet eleven in the morning, and I have gone from freezing my ass off to sweating to freezing my ass off and then to sweating again. I've taken two showers, been crushed by Logatelli, been treated for fungus, blown through an unsanitary musical instrument, and now I'm supposed to eat hamburger meat from yesterday's sloppy joes. My legs are badly burned, and I am tired. And there is still the prospect of frog dissection.

On that front, the girls are all in a lather. Frogs are the talk of the lunchroom, and everyone is yapping about it as I go to my next class, which is called, strangely, *Health*. That is the catchall term for everything from sex ed to malaria prevention to making pancakes. Don't ask me why, but health class is taught by a rotating group of gym teachers. That makes sense to someone somewhere, as does the fact that the course also covers driver's ed. Our teacher for the driver's ed unit is—you guessed it—the wrestling-obsessed Mr. Lambert. He doesn't like to talk much off the mat, so he just shows us movies. Today's is *The Smith Method of Space Cushion Driving*. Some guy named Smith drives around in a '57 Pontiac convertible demonstrating his revolutionary style of driving, which mainly consists of giving the guy ahead of you some room. That's the big deal: don't tailgate. But the hilarious thing is Smith is talking to the camera the whole time. At one point, he almost smashes into a guy in a Plymouth making a left. I look around to see if anyone else is catching this, but the whole room is asleep—tough to stay awake after spaghetti.

Then we go to the much-anticipated sixth-period class, biology. We sit at black plastic lab tables that have holes in the middle, which I suppose are there in case we need to build something requiring a large cylindrical tube. Our teacher is Mr. Palmer, a creepy guy who is like six foot five. He is incredibly psyched to be at the frog-dissection part of the year. He gives us a big speech about the importance of what we are about to do, like we're astronauts or something.

"I have come to see frog dissection as a rite of passage for children in the public-school system," he says. "Your time in school can be remembered in two distinct sections—dissected, if you will. There are your childhood years before you dissect a frog. At this point, you are young and immature—some of you very much so. Your bodies are not yet developed. Your minds are simple."

He begins to go around the room, handing out the poor frogs for us to cut up. They are in vacuum-packed plastic wrappers. "Then, after frog dissection, you become young adults. You become worldlier, more experienced. Your bodies open like flowers. You begin to get complicated. You perspire more readily…"

He comes to me and Ernie first. Out of nowhere, a plan comes to me. I stick our frog in the drawer underneath the lab table. I say, "We didn't get ours."

"I didn't give you one?"

"No."

"I could've sworn I gave you one."

"No, Mr. Palmer. I'm really looking forward to it, and we didn't get one yet."

"Sorry about that," he says and gives us a second frog.

Ernie says, "What the hell are you doing?"

I stare at him and say, "Don't worry about it. This has nothing to do with you."

After about fifteen minutes of introductory dissection, I ask to go to the bathroom. Mr. Palmer gives me his signature hall pass, an igneous rock with a home-drilled hole for the piece of rope through which the bathroom-bound student puts his or her hand. Nutball. I put the shrink-wrapped amphibian in my shirtsleeve, having finally found a use for that button between the wrist and the elbow. It's perfect for keeping a dead frog.

You can only get away with about eight minutes on a bathroom pass from Mr. Palmer, so I know I have to move fast. I book over to A wing in three minutes and find my target: the water fountain in the middle of the hallway. I rip open the plastic packaging and place my little green friend right in the center of the drain. Thinking of Jim Brown in *The Dirty Dozen*, I make sure the coast is clear and get back to class.

Twenty minutes later, I sit down as cool as a cucumber in study hall. Liz walks in just as the bell sounds.

"What's up, Biz?" That's what I call her.

"Not much. I hate my mom." She talks to me about her family a lot.

"Oh no. Something happen?"

"No. She's just a crazy French shrew."

"At least she's interesting."

"What do you mean?"

"I don't know. I mean, don't you think sometimes that we're in this, like, crazy-boring, postsixties malaise of consumerism and cultural vacuity that threatens our sanity? I know it makes me crazy."

She stares at me for a while. Then, in a way she's never spoken to me before, she says, "What are you going to *be*, Roman?"

"I don't know. But whatever it is, it wouldn't stop me from doing anything for you."

21

Right on time, there is a long tone from the intercom speaker next to the clock, which means someone is being requested by the principal's office. It's like a walkie-talkie system between the front lines and central command. A voice comes on.

"Mrs. Warden, please send Roman Budding to see Mr. Fertel. Immediately."

I'm on my feet before she finishes. My look tells Mrs. Warden that handcuffs will not be necessary. Liz, who looks a little baffled by the end of our conversation, watches me.

I usually talk to Mr. Fertel about baseball. He has a bad back, and he walks stooped over with his right hand lifted a little. He looks kind of like a chicken when I walk in. He's sitting on the ground with his back against the wall. He's famous for that. It makes his back feel better.

"What the hell's wrong with you?" he says.

"I'm sorry."

He starts to get up, but he can't. At first, I think, "Wow, he is in bad shape." Then I realize he's cracking up. Hysterical. Can't stop laughing. His secretary, Mrs. Shinglehoffer, walks in. She's laughing, too. She helps him up and steadies him to his chair, and then she leaves.

He tries to get serious. "Ok, dipshit. What possessed you to do something like that? I have to punish you, you know."

"It just happened," I say. "I can't explain it."

"All right," he says. He ponders me for a second. "Roman, try to use your powers for good and not evil."

"Huh?"

"Never mind. You have two weeks of detention starting today. And I'm calling your mother."

As I walk out, Mrs. Shinglehoffer motions me over. She looks around and whispers, "Did you hear what happened?"

"No, Mrs. Shinglehoffer."

"Ed Lutz was the first one to the water fountain." She's whispering, but she can't stop laughing. "He freaked out...and then..."

"What? Mrs. Shinglehoffer?"

"He...he crapped himself. Poor soul..." She grabs a tissue.

Once I get out of there, I head to my locker. Liz is waiting for me with Jane and a couple of other girls. "I heard all about it, you idiot," Liz says.

"Pretty good, Roman," says Jane.

"Are you suspended?" Liz asks.

"Nah, just detention for two weeks."

Jane whispers something to her, and she and the other girls walk away. Liz starts to drift away with them but lingers for a second.

"Are you taking the sports bus, then?" she says.

I have a fit of overeager doofiness. "Yeah, I guess so. That's at four, right? Is that the bus you take? Oh right, you have cheerleading practice."

"Usually. If I don't go to Jane's. Maybe I'll see you on the bus."

And then she's gone.

And now I'm here, with all the AC/DC fans and Mr. Matthews, who says we can leave ten minutes early. I think he's got somewhere to go. God knows what that guy does.

———

Well, I never thought I'd come back to this, but times change. I'm in my room and it's late. Before I go to sleep, I might as well finish this story.

I get to the four-o'clock sports bus, and at first it looks like Liz won't make it. I'm feeling stupid for thinking I was getting somewhere with her. But just as the bus pulls away, she pops up the steps, heads right over to my seat, and says, "Move over, buster."

As we ride, she tells me of the status of the cheer-leading team's repertoire, which is more interesting than you might think. When she finishes, she says, "I cannot believe you did that with the frogs. That's the most wicked funny thing that's happened all year."

"Aw, you know. Any chance to get back at them."

"Very immature. I love it." Then she looks at me curiously and says, "You could get into big trouble, you know." And she gives me a friendly push. It's new, this idea of her touching me. I try to stay calm. "Hey," she says, "do you want to come over for a while?"

Her house is one of those huge nice places with the flowers everywhere and the circular driveway, which I guess, theoretically, is for chauffeurs to drop people off, except these houses aren't that fancy. You go into one of these places and it's like the ceilings and the walls are bigger, like it holds more life or something. Definitely a place where you can get away from one another—unlike Stuckley, where we live like Japanese people getting on the subway.

I get in the house, and her mom is, like, the prettiest woman I've ever seen. Her name is Carolina, which doesn't sound that French to me, so someone in their family must be from Spain. Like her daughter, she has thick black hair, which is pulled back by a red and white polka-dot barrette. She's wearing a super-cool black dress. I guess Liz' hips are from the old man's side, because her mom is really thin. That may cause some problems later in life between mother and child, but that's a whole other road. Mrs. Tremblay looks a hell of a lot different than my mom, I'll tell you that.

"Where do you live, Romahn?" she asks. I love the way she pronounces my name, like I'm an Italian card player.

"We live in Stuckley, Mrs. Tremblay."

"What is Stuckley? What is zees, Lizbet?"

Liz rolls her eyes. "Mama. It is the place by the mall. Where you like to go for the cheeseburgers."

"Oh, yes, yes. Where zey have Burger King and toolayshows." I don't know what "toolayshows" are, but Liz does, and she nods.

"Mama, we're going into the den."

"Do you want chocalat?" asks Mrs. Tremblay.

It takes me a minute before I realize she is offering us hot chocolate. We stay in the kitchen as she makes it. Liz gets annoyed and looks at the crossword puzzle her father left incomplete on the table. Mrs. Tremblay is drinking a glass of red wine she poured from a bottle with a cork. I make small talk, but there are moments when it's impossible to understand her. Liz chimes in when I need bailing out. I ask for the bathroom, and there are two toilets in there. One just has a faucet in the middle — I don't know what the hell these people do with that. I make a decision and go American.

We get our hot chocolate and go into the den, which is a big room with tons of books, a piano, two couches, a coffee table, white marble ashtray, and a deep-brown shag carpet. It looks more like a place to have tea with the Black Panthers than a place for kids to hang out. We plop down on the couch, and Liz sits facing me with her back against the arm and her legs crossed in front of her.

"Let me read your palm," she says, reaching out to grab my hand. I shift toward her till I am up against her legs. I'm still trying to stay calm, trying to not think about where I am right now and the eight thousand ways I can make a goddamn fool of myself with one wrong move.

"Your life line is long…" She is really focused, like a doctor going over an X-ray. "But something happens right here, in the middle." She holds my palm up to my face. I have no idea what she's talking about. Me, Roman Budding, confused by two beautiful French women within twenty minutes. More importantly, though, the reading is finished, and it's not clear where, exactly, my hand should go. Right then and there, I realize I don't know how much longer I can live with myself without at least *trying* something. So I interlace my fingers with hers.

She doesn't scream. In fact, she seems to be fine with it. We sit there and don't say anything for a while. I can't resist rubbing my thumb up and down her ring finger once, but I stop because I don't want to call too much attention to the fact that she is holding hands with me. I'm scared she will wake up any second, come to her senses, and pull her hand away. But she doesn't.

She breaks the silence by pointing at my jeans. "What happened?" My pant leg has run up, and the burns can be seen.

"Oh God. Wrestling," I say.

"What do you mean?" She is giggling a little, which is very cute.

"Ugh. It's the worst. Getting smothered by Peter Logatelli trying to sit-out."

"How do your legs get burnt?"

I look around and see an opening on the shag beyond the coffee table. "Here, let me show you." She follows me over to the carpet. "Ok, you're me and I'm Peter. You start off like this." I show her how to take the bottom position, on hands and knees. Then I loop my arm under her waist and hold her left arm above the wrist. She smells incredibly great. She has a green sweater made out of fancy wool, which is softer than my pillow. It bunches up above her waist and I can see the top of her panties: orange and very distracting. They're sticking out of her corduroys, which are a different color green and go nicely with the sweater and her flowered shirt. And, of course, I look real quick at her butt, the derriere extraordinaire.

"When the whistle blows, you're supposed to stick your right leg out like this." I guide her hips very gently to show her the proper form of a sit-out. "Then you just sit down. On your butt. There." And with that, she's sitting, facing away from me. A perfect sit-out. I am on my knees behind her with my arms around her waist.

She turns her head. "Like that?"

Her face is right in front of me. I kiss her. It's easier than saying hi in the morning or trying to think of how to make her laugh in study hall; easier than trying to find her alone at her locker; easier than saying the right thing to Jane, hoping she will relay it to Liz; and it's easier than sticking a frog in my shirt. It's the easiest thing in the world.

"Show me again," she says and gets back on her hands and knees.

Once we are in position, I say, "Wait for the whistle." She thinks this is funny. She tells me I am tickling her.

"Lizbet! Romahn! What ze hell are you doing?" It's her mom. She's one big flambé of cigarette smoke, polka dots, and red wine. She is mad and more confused than we are.

After a few awkward moments trying to explain American wrestling and why such a thing would be practiced in the public schools, Carolina starts to come around. I even show her my burnt shins in an effort to dig myself out. But I think the sight of me pulling up my jeans is the last straw because she says, "Ok, well, Romahn, you are a very nize boy. *Très* funny. But I sink it iz time for you to go, *non?*"

She offers to drive me home, but I say *non*. "But, you live, like, four miles from here," Liz says.

I am pretty touched that she can even estimate it. "It's two point six miles, actually," I say. "But I'll be fine. I like to walk." I don't exactly want to get in a car with Mrs. Tremblay, and neither, I assume, does Liz, who shrugs and then smiles at me before I go.

Blackhorse Pike, the road back to my house, starts as a little street and becomes a two-lane highway. It grew to service the fancy developments out here in the suburbs. There are two bright-yellow lines in the middle that occasionally become broken to indicate where fast cars may pass slower ones. The road goes up hills and around banks, through woods and past shopping centers. I watch the cars going by and wonder what Mr. Smith would say about their spacing.

When I get to an open stretch near Ridley Creek State Park, I stop. I just stand there, looking at the sky. I don't know what time it is. I stand on Blackhorse Pike for I don't know how long — probably twenty minutes. The day is gone, and it's getting cold as hell.

I think about guiding her hips through a sit-out. I start walking again. I think about her sweater and her lips. I still smell her. I start to run. Slowly at first, kind of a home-run trot. Then I go faster. Then faster still. All the way home.

Slipstream

They say a judge is a lawyer who knows a politician and a federal judge is a lawyer who knows a senator, and so it was for Murphy, who went to law school with Cranston, who got elected after Watergate and promptly gave his old buddy the first seat he controlled. That was in the year of our Lord 1974.

Klezak stands now in Murphy's marble-encrusted courtroom on Hill Street in downtown LA, with its dark walnut benches, gray carpet, and United States seal. There are microphones at the two podiums where the attorneys present argument. It is Monday, motion day. Klezak is next to the big firm lawyer, Stetson, who has the preliminary ruling—written by Murphy's clerk, a Persian from Stanford—in his favor. Murphy is bored.

"Do you have a rebuttal?" asks the judge.

Klezak stammers through a protest about contractual interpretation being for the jury and not the court, and Murphy lets him finish. Stetson knows a good thing when he sees it and, when it's his turn, has nothing to add, ensuring his victory, which Murphy confirms in a tired voice, reading a slipstream of language to the court reporter, which will be repeated into the boilerplate appellate clerks use to burn the case into law.

Klezak gets in the car and inserts his earpiece. He calls the assistant vice president for claims at State Farm to report the beating, but she is out just now, so he leaves word. Klezak already knows he is not going back to the office. He has worked sixteen days straight and twenty-seven days total this month, answering interrogatories, propounding document requests, conducting document review, Bates-stamping evidence, reading deposition transcripts, writing motions to compel, opposition briefs, jury instructions, and orders to show cause. As he drives, another case dead in the water, he feels it coming.

At Wilshire and La Brea, he goes left, then left again on Cabezilla to his house. The grass is the color of hay, like Wyeth grass. Inside it is dark, as it always is, because he thinks darkness keeps the house cool in the long, flat, dry afternoons. He removes his glasses at the bathroom sink and looks at his face. It keeps on coming. He decides he will take the day. He goes to the garage, stuffed with horded junk so voluminous he can't fit the car, and next to the hot-water heater finds the cardboard box. The flap says *Service 9-01; repair Inlet Gauge, monitor regulator.* The box contains black pants and a white button-up shirt, both layered with filmy grime like that of a restaurant floor.

Beside the box is a grease pan he keeps for these occasions. He dabs a finger in it and begins to smear his neck, taking care not to mar the skin too badly while still filling the pores with jet-black. He rubs the thick, oozy emollient through his hair until it gets stringy. He begins changing into the clothes. He shuts his eyes when he breathes in the body odor of the shirt. He feels the blood in his temple as he gets ready to go. His mind begins to loosen when he starts the car.

"Klezak, you fuck," he says. It is a mutter, and it becomes steady as he backs the car out the driveway. "Murphy, fuck you. Jack-off. Never been a good judge. Fat, lazy fuck. Depends on the clerks, anyway. It's hourly, anyway. Will send the fucking bill, anyway. Let them move the file. Let someone else deal with that Stetson." He speaks in a loud voice now. "You're dealing with a rich plaintiff, Holly. Ms. State Farm. Fuck you. A fucking plaintiff who can pay a big fancy lawyer, Holly. When the rich man is plaintiff, you're fucked in the ass." At the light, he pulls at his hair and holds his dirty palms to his cheeks. "Fucked in the ass, Holly." He drives on. He squeezes the wheel. "Klezak, you *fuck*. You do the discovery and then you get removed. Klezak fuck. Klezak fuck."

La Brea is crowded, but when he gets on the I-10, he sails. He gets off at Fourth Street in Santa Monica, where he drives into the Sears lot. The Sears is old, like a throwback, like the sixties or the fifties, a timeless place with women in girdles and those white sunglasses with the points, the Flannery O'Connor kind. He goes down the escalator to the Home and Garden section. The green hoses smell like rubbery-flavored water, the kind you get when you put your lips up to the brass end. "Breach of contract for the jury," he says. He is spitting his words. "Fuck you. I lick that metal when I drink from a hose. Stick my tongue inside and roll it all around."

He hears a voice: "Welcome to Sears. Let me know if I can help you find anything." It's a black girl with a weight problem. She wears braces, the kind with double rubber bands connecting the molars.

"I'm fine," he snaps. "I don't need any help. I'm fine."
She smiles at him. "The hoses are on sale."

"I don't *want* any help," he says.

"Ok, sir. Let me know if you need anything."

"*Sir?*" he yells "*Sir*, my ass. Don't give me your bullshit.
Get out of this section. Go back to the kitchen sale. Go
upstairs to the fucking women's clothes. Get your fat black
ass out of here and up to the women's clothes."

She steps back. She is a nice girl, now sad and upset
at the vulgarity directed her way, not the kind who fights
back, or files a civil rights case.

"This is how it comes," Klezak yells at her, moving away.
She lingers a second and looks at him, but he has
headed on, over to Automotive. There are dozens of tires
stacked. He runs his fingers over the white circumferential
line of a steel-belted Michelin. More rubber. "Rubber
is what you want from a fucking Sears." He breathes in
deep. "So clean now." He opens his eyes, angry now. "Not
the rotten smell. Not the rotten smell of fucking burning
tire piles where it will end. Fucking burning fucking tire
piles where it will end. Fucking fire." He looks for the exit.
"Fucking fire and fire and fire and burning, burning smell."

He follows Broadway down to Ocean and gets out
on the grass of the park paralleling the beach. By one of
the palms, he closes his eyes again. He feels the grease
on his face and hair and presses his hands into the grimy
legs of his pants, which have the color and texture of
trampled gum on high school hallway floors. "Klezak
fuck." He opens his eyes. "Klezak fuuuuuuuck." He is
yelling it louder now. He heads north on the walkway,
dodging skaters and couples. He pays no attention to the
shadowy bums lying on the grass and next to the trees,

the sunburned, drunken homeless. He faces the ocean just beyond the statue of Santa Monica, at the fence that guards pedestrians from the cliffs overlooking the beach. "Please let it come now," he says. He starts to loosen.

He focuses first on the horizon and talks to it. "Where do you think this came from, this notion of harmony? Do you think it came from God or from some other source? Do you think it is right and just? Do you think it is *just* that this happens? That these fucking monkeys get it and you get nothing?"

The icy feeling is receding. His stomach, so sour and grinding all morning, is of no bother. He picks up the pace. "You and your *goddamn* money, thinking it is so much. I will tell you one thing: you don't bring it to me or to *America* and think that there is nothing to do. You can't do that, man. You can't do that without hearing from me. I will speak for the people."

A runner comes down the path as Klezak approaches Colorado. An older, trim, and suntanned man, he looks like Stetson. As he bears down on Klezak, the Stetson runner makes eye contact.

"Is there something? Is there something you want?" says Klezak. The Stetson runner breezes by. "Get out of my *goddamn way*!" Klezak screams. The man looks back and gives a little grin.

Klezak turns right at the light at Colorado and glides onto the Third Street Promenade. He scours left and right for targets, but slowly the monologue takes hold again. He arrives at the intersection of Santa Monica and the Promenade. It is still early. Passersby move east and west, going for bargain movie show times or burgers or to buy Gap T-shirts. He prowls. It is an old, worn groove. He begins to yell. "It all starts with the Bible, you stupid motherfuckers. That was the basis. Hamilton, Jefferson, Adams...*Washington*, you idiots. All before you get to anything else. You don't know Thoreau; you don't know Aquinas. You don't know Steiner and Kafka. You don't even know *that*. You don't even know what it *means* to be *living*. You are ants, you are caterpillars, you are *fucking insects*."

———

My name is Torres, and I am a Santa Monica cop. "Only you, Torres—only you could get this one," Noah said when I turned it in. Marcello Noah—100 percent prick. I asked him what kind of cop has a twenty-four-foot fishing boat in San Pedro. "Dude," he said, "my name is Noah." He used to do the same beat as me when I was new to SMPD. But he had a lot of seniority, and one day I look up and he's been bumped up to sergeant. I guess he saved his money, and with lots of OT, lots of benefits, who knows? He managed his shit. Good for him. I know he thought I was soft. But that's another story.

Ten years ago, it became obvious that the Third Street Promenade—the big commercial area downtown—was a problem for us, logistically speaking. We couldn't take a patrol car in there because it is a crowded walk street. When we drove a unit on the walkway—it's a big walkway—everybody freaked out. That meant we had no clear way to get the bad guys and the nuts and the bums in line, always stopping on Santa Monica or Broadway and jamming up traffic.

So they decide to put us on foot, in shorts and golf shirts. Except not exactly golf shirts—bigger, big enough to put the vests under. Anyway, it becomes obvious that that's not going to work. Let's imagine that an incident goes down on, say, Wilshire, and we're over on Broadway. Now we got to run down the fucking Promenade, all *Five-O*, blazing through like maniacs. Gives you two problems: one, we've got everyone on the streets all freaked out again; and two, we're *running. Oyame, chico.* We could be a quarter mile or a half mile away from that call, and we'd have to all run down through the crowd, getting everyone crazy watching the chase. And then what? Be so tired we're worthless whenever we get to the perp? Pretty soon there's a complaint from ten people who say we smashed into them running by, and the city council starts saying it's really dangerous. Next thing you know, nobody's shopping, and it's all our fault, yada yada.

Point is we ended up on bikes. Bicycles. The union stopped it at first, but then some guys — and this included me — said, "What the fuck?" It made us more mobile, and once we saw that the bikes weren't so bad looking — they were black and kind of cool — we got on board. And there we were: on the bikes patrolling Third Street. Better than trolling around all day in a worn-out unit with some nutsack. And I'm still in Santa Monica, *entiendes*? It's safer being a cop here than teaching social studies at Crenshaw.

When you cover the TSP in the morning on the bikes, it's kind of peaceful. You want to let the driver on the street cleaner get done, or if you have to be out there, you stay clear. I like to think of the Promenade as my beat, my neighborhood, like an old-school cop. I talk to regular people: waitresses, kids who make the drinks at Starbucks, and the trash guys. Due respect, they let too many low-end retail places come in, like bad stores with slutty clothes and Foot Locker. Doesn't make sense to me that they don't put in upscale stores like Gucci, Dolce, and shit like Whole Foods. A better class of people would follow. But what do I know?

The day I'm talking about, I'm moving along from the Broadway Deli up to Borders, where I usually stop in to look at the books, read magazines a little, and get some coffee. There's a girl working there with orange streaks in her hair and a nose ring; she's a good kid. We're catching up, saying hi and whatnot, when I hear yelling. I head out. It's a guy, who I figure is from a shelter, looking pretty rough, on a rant.

He's all "Insects—you're all a bunch of insects." He's screaming it. You have to be careful with that profile; when someone begins yelling in a street, it's a sign that they've lost touch with the rules that govern people. This one looks like a typical tinfoil-glasses, the End is Near type. We get them often in the morning. High percentage of psychotics. The drunks sleep late; the ones walking around and yelling before lunchtime are usually pretty far gone. PSs—paranoid schizophrenics. Referential mania, too. Really jumpy.

It was right at noon, so I can't rule out that he's a drunk or a junky. He shut up once he saw me riding over. I put the bike against the bench. "Good morning," I say. He backs up against the wall of the J. Crew. Almost puts his fucking hands up. He stinks like b.o., but not like alcohol. Loud and clear, I say, "How are you today, sir?"

"I'm fine," he says.

"Well," I say, "you're making a lot of noise. You're yelling, sir. Do you know that?" There was no response. "Have you been drinking?"

"No."

I poke around him a little, getting closer to smell him again. Still he stinks but no booze, so what he says about drinking appears to be true. This presents a problem for me, because to send him away with more than a ticket—say, a PC 647—instead of just writing him up for a PC 415 disturbing the peace, he needs to be visibly intoxicated. And even for a section 415 I have to see an actual fight, an unreasonably loud noise, or something intended to provoke an immediate violent reaction. You wouldn't believe the shit I've taken from judges not being able to put a bum on one of those three.

"Where you staying?" I say.

"SA."

That dampens my desire to bust him even more. We get lots of nuts out of the Salvation Army on Fifth Street. Cots, no toilet seats, stabbings, hypodermic needles. PSs, drunks, junkies. I think about it. My shift is almost over, so I can be back to the station soon, turn in the bike, and be on the way to the gym and then home within an hour. Plus, truth is that I don't want to put this guy down. His face has something about it. The eyes are clear. That you never see: clear eyes. He's dirty— like greasy dirty—and his skin and clothes are covered in the kind of scum you get sleeping in driveways and bushes. But this guy does not have that dark red-brown color the real drunks get—the ones who've spent twenty or thirty days at the beach all day and night, just taking breaks to get loaded or find the soup kitchen. The true homeless have a deep sunburn that tells their story better than any ID card or medical records I ever saw.

I make a decision. "Why don't you head back that way, sir?" I say. "And no more yelling. If I have to run you down again because you're yelling at people, I'm gonna put you in jail, you understand me?"

"Yes, officer," he says.

"Ok," I say, "don't let me hear about you."

———

Torres finishes his shift and changes his clothes at the precinct headquarters adjacent to city hall, site of the O.J. Simpson civil trial and the steady stream of court appearances of pop stars busted for drunk driving. Torres gets in his truck. He stops at the light coming out of the Civic Center, at the entrance to the freeway. To his left, a man sits in a Lexus with sunglasses and a baseball cap over long hair, waiting for the arrow to go onto the highway. Torres squints. There is a glare against the windshield from the LA sun that overexposes the image for a moment, and it doesn't make sense. Here is a very dirty man in a nice car. Then the light softens, and suddenly everything becomes clear.

"Holy shit," Torres says out loud to no one.

Torres follows Klezak down the I-10 freeway for several miles to Overland and eventually to a high-rise in Century City. Torres checks the office listings, and after he shows his badge to the guards, he makes it to the thirty-third floor. The receptionist gets the same badge flashed to her, and Torres walks through the offices one by one.

Klezak is sitting behind his desk when Torres comes in. He looks as though he were expecting the cop.

"You found me," Klezak says.

"Yes, I did," says Torres, slowly crossing the threshold. They look at each other in silence. Torres can see no trace of Klezak's dirty skin and clothes. His hair is slicked back and conforms with the office environment — long but not too long. With a shirt and tie, he looks normal.

"What now?" says Klezak.

"I don't know. Can I sit down?"

"Please." Klezak gestures at the chair in front of his desk. A few bad pictures hang on the walls, a lamp sits on the corner of the lawyer's desk, and stacks of paper crowd the corners.

Torres sits and stares at Klezak, whose face, shirt, and blue-and-white-striped tie explode at him in their nattiness, their Pentecostalness — none of it has a speck of dirt.

"You followed me," says Klezak.

"Yes, I did."

"Well, what can I do for you? Should we discuss this morning?"

Torres studies his eyes, looking for signs of mania, paranoia, or danger. There are none. He does not know what to make of this strange, sad man. "Well, first, just tell me…man, are you…like, ok? It's a little scary."

"I'm fine, Officer Torres. I'm not homeless. I work in this office. I have my own practice. I'm just a lawyer." He smiles. "And I did nothing illegal. You and I both know that."

Torres takes this in. "You were close." He waits for a reaction. "I could have written you up easy. Sent you away for the seventy-two-hour dry out."

Klezak is unfazed.

"It's really weird," Torres says finally. "You have to admit that."

"Maybe so," says Klezak. Then, in an instant, he seems to lose his confidence, as though revealing a bluff. "I can't keep paying you guys. My deal was that I'd only have to pay once for the whole force."

Torres thinks for a second and then nods. "Noah."

Klezak doesn't respond.

"This is how Noah got the boat, right?" Torres says. "The one in Long Beach. We could never figure that out."

Klezak offers a small, nervous smile. "A boat is what he wanted."

Torres stares more. Klezak is serene again, caught but not guilty.

Suddenly Torres has a feeling he does not recognize. A powerful sense of being swept away. He blinks his eyes, but nothing changes. Now there is a buttery yellow light behind Klezak's head. Torres stands and moves a few steps to see if it is an illusion.

"But you're not Noah," says Klezak as Torres moves. "We both know that."

Torres continues walking, circling Klezak at his desk. The light stays above the lawyer's head. Torres goes back to his seat.

"I'm really starting to lose it," Torres says.

"No, you're not," says Klezak. His voice is soothing. "You're waking up."

"But Noah...Noah's fine. He just took the money and went back to work?"

Klezak says, "Noah could not see it."

Torres considers this, and in doing so he feels hopeful and then excited. Then he starts to relax, like a patient who has just taken a needle. "Maybe so."

Klezak gets up from behind the desk and walks to Torres at his seat. The light remains. He extends his hand to Torres, who takes it and rises. Klezak's secretary, well trained, comes to the threshold and closes the door.

"Will you pray with me, Eddie?" says Klezak.

"How'd you know my name?"

"I know a lot more than that."

The light is fuller now. Klezak's eyes are a deep blue. The two bow their heads against their interlocked fingers. Torres closes his eyes, and in his earthly eyelids he sees light, followed by an open field. He knows he is in the presence of angels. "It is here for me," he thinks. It is a transcendent, translucent feeling, the God of the preachers, the long-held power of his native soul. He opens his eyes.

"Will you follow me?" says Klezak.

Here Comes Mike

1.

If you go back through the tunnel of time to when basketball was holy, you will find that Mike Donegan scored thirty-six points against Cardinal O'Hara in the Southeastern Pennsylvania Diocese championship game of 1966. He took over in the last five minutes, with clutch buckets, bruising defense, and a coast-to-coast three-point play that lit up the gym, got the bench dancing, and made his coach, Brother Francis, close his eyes and punch the air.

Mike was the best player in the history of Nativity BVM Junior High. It was not just that he could shoot and was a step faster; it was his personality. Like any great ballplayer—any truly great player—he was emotionally detached, a bit of an asshole on the court. He had no choke in him. In close games against Saint James and Archbishop Prendergast or when they played public schools like Media or Eddystone, or even against the all-black teams from Chester, as the game wore down, the crowd, the scorekeepers, and the janitors would say quietly to themselves, like a pious flock, "Here comes Mike."

John and his mother and sisters went to every game, sitting on old bleachers in church gyms with half-moon backboards and floors of loose wood or even cement or tile. Snack stands served red licorice, Bazooka bubblegum, and hot dogs boiled in plain pots of water. The snackstand ladies wore double-knit cardigans from Sears, and their giant bosoms hit the heads of any five-year-olds standing too close. When they talked it was to say things like: "'Scuse me, hon," and "You need another quarter, love," and "You can't take that soda in the gym." John's job was counting Mike's points.

Margie starting asking him, "How many does he have now, Jackie?" for the first time in the third quarter of the O'Hara game early in the season. Everyone got into it as the games went by. "How many does he have, Jackie?" they would yell. His brother wanted the ball any time it mattered. On wintery playgrounds anywhere in the Diocese, as imaginary clocks ticked down in imaginary games, boys pretended to be Mike Donegan taking it to the house.

Mike was the oldest of Mickey and Rosemary Donegan's five children, followed by Donny; the two girls, Annemarie and Margie; and John. Nine years from oldest to youngest, the difference between growing up in the sixties and the seventies. Rosemary Donegan loved all her kids, but Mike was her angel from God. Before church on Sunday, she stood in front with a trash can and collected food for the orphanage at Saint Ignatius. The priests knew she brought in more than anyone else in the parish. She was beautiful, with thick black hair, thin features, and a curvy cupcake of a body, which, in light of her five kids, must have been a reward from the saints.

She was urgently, passionately Catholic, saying the Rosary every day and novenas twice a month. She was a barrel of energy, going to mass at half past five and forever visiting aunts in nursing homes. Part and parcel went a sense of doom. Rosemary could not watch the kids' games or even the Eagles or the Phillies when things got too close, hiding her eyes or sneaking looks at the television from behind the wall. She put sugar in spaghetti sauce and salt on her oatmeal.

Her kids loved her first above all other things. She had a special language with each, private and kind; a dialogue about bodies, clothes, schedules, favorite colors, and things wanted most for Christmas. And with Mike, whom she could not take her eyes off since the day he was born, she had quiet conversations and shared the gentle connection between Irish mother and son that ran all the way through the ages, all the way down to the sad, stubborn, and reluctantly consecrated core.

John never forgot waiting with his mother on a cold Friday night for his father to get home from the police station. Mike had been caught drinking behind the Lenni Firehouse with his cousin Peter. Annemarie was just about to put John to bed when their father's sister, Aunt Marian called.

"Mickey, the boys are in jail," she said.

"What the hell are you talking about?" said Mickey.

"Peter and Mike. The state cops just called. You have to go get them. They're at the station on Route 352. Hurry."

"Christ, Marian, they're fifteen."

Times changed. Mike lost interest in sports, feeling the natural order of things drawing him toward steel-toe boots and flannel shirts. He spent most of his time in fields and in cars smoking pot. He smoked big fat bowls of ragweed homegrown dope that burned the throat and caused him to not care about basketball or college or Bobby Kennedy. He started hanging around a girl named Ginny DiMeo, who dressed the same way he did and always seemed to have a runny nose whenever she came over to the Donegans' house. One night before bed, John heard Donny tell Annemarie that Peter told him Mike had licked Vicki DiMeo's tits in the woods by the football field at the high school.

After Mickey drove away, the four younger kids and their mother did not speak, as though talking would bring bad luck. They were all the same, the other Donegans, besides Mickey and Mike. Taking Rosemary's lead, they worried for the world and obsessed over the oldest son, the big brother, who was a broad canvas on which they painted all their fears. There were differences, but they were the subtle differences between apples from the same tree. Donny had a bad temper. Annemarie had red hair and Rosemary's big hips and love of rosary beads. Margie was dark; she was the one the boys liked. John was the youngest but the smartest, separated somehow. Even then, when he was six years old, the family knew, with a strange, unspoken clairvoyance, that he would leave.

Though Mike was quiet, he was unfailingly nice to John, even as he became alienated and silent when at home. Mike never did well at school, but Rosemary could not discipline him, leaving enforcement of rules as a matter between father and son. Mickey Donegan was a simple guy, a plumber who liked a sandwich and a shot and a beer. Even before his first arrest behind the firehouse, Mickey was convinced the kid would go wrong. Truth be told, he preferred his daughters.

The Pontiac parked at the curb, and Mike got out of the passenger's side. "Oh thank God," Rosemary said to the other kids. "Here comes Mike." John looked out the front side window of the family's row home to see if his father's grip on Mike's collar was the painful kind or the loving kind. It was actually not so tight—not the kind that said "get the fuck in the house"—and John could tell that Mickey was relieved. But by the time they got through the door, Mickey's anger had risen. Rosemary ran to them, all hustle and bustle, and said, "Michael Christopher, are you ok? What in God's name were you doing?"

"He's fine," said Mickey. "But he's a dumb son of a bitch. And he's gonna be a tired son of a bitch, too."

Mike's eyes were glassy, and he was maybe a touch wobbly, but he was peaceful. If he was scared, John couldn't see it. His hands were bleeding.

Mickey continued in a raised voice, "With the fine and court costs, it was one hundred and thirty-three bucks."

"Oh Jesus," said Rosemary. "Michael."

"A dollar an hour. That's what it's gonna be, pal," said Mickey. "One hundred and thirty-three hours of work for me. I know your math's not too good, so I've done the calculations for you. It starts tomorrow and will go every day till it's worked off."

"What happened to your hands?" said Rosemary. Mike seemed not to know. "Go to your room and get washed up. I'll get you a bandage."

"A dollar an hour. Add it up," said Mickey.

"The rest of you get to bed, too," said Rosemary. "Jackie, you should have been in bed hours ago. Annemarie, I told you to put him to bed."

The kids shared the second floor and its bathroom. Their parents had the stuffy third-floor bedroom that sat atop the small house like the bridge of a ship. John peeked in on Mike, who was in the room he shared with Donny. Mike had stripped down to his boxers and was lying in bed, wrapping ACE bandages around his hands.

"You ok?" asked John.

"I'm ok."

"Did you really get arrested?"

"Kind of," Mike said. But then he said, "Just got into a little hot water, Jack boy. It'll blow over."

"Are you going to go to jail?"

Mike laughed. "No way, José. Cops just try to scare ya."

"Why didn't you run?" said Donny.

"You can't run, Donny," said Mike. "You can't just *run*."

"What happened to your hands?" said Donny.

"Cop did it. After they put us in the car. He picked up one of the broken beer bottles we'd chucked at the wall. He told me to open my hands, and then he put a piece of glass in each one and said, 'Make a fist.'"

"Jesus," said Donny.

"Mommy was scared," said John. "She was crying."

"She was?" Mike said. "Just forget about that."

"Ok."

"All right. Go to bed, man, ok?"

John closed the door and heard Margie and Annemarie in the bathroom. "C'mon. Move," said Annemarie. "Daddy's coming up. I have to brush my teeth."

John headed to the girls' bedroom, which was his room also, until a few years later when Mike got drafted. John climbed into Annemarie's bed instead of his own little cot, and when she returned from the bathroom, she pulled him in close under the covers, like she did on most nights, too tired to put him back where he belonged.

2.

Rosemary died in February 1971 from primary brain cancer. She went fast. "Astro-site-toma, grade four," John heard the nurse say during one visit to the hospital, which stuck in his head because he was in fourth grade and it made him think of the Astrodome. She slept all the time at the end. John worried that she wouldn't wake up to say good-bye to him as time was running out. But she did. A few hours before she passed, she held his face and said, "Jackie, my big strong man, you know what you have inside of you. Take care of your brothers and sisters."

At the funeral, John followed along in between Donny and Margie. A young nun sang "Ave Maria," standing black-and-white in the knave in front of the stained-glass explosions of the apostles. Mike was sent back from the army just in time to say good-bye, and John watched him from across the pew and in front of the grave. He tried to hold Mike's hand when he could during each of the processions of the day: from the church to the cars, from the cars to the gravesite, from the gravesite to the cars. When he couldn't be with Mike, he held Margie's or Annemarie's hand instead, letting go only to grab their shoulders if their heads went down to cry.

3.

Thirty-five years later, John boarded the Metroliner in Penn Station on a Saturday morning in fall. It had the makings of a good football day, and a conflicting, crisp mood took over Manhattan as he left. John thought of the Bloody Marys he was missing in the parking lot at Columbia, where his friends from business school would be before the Cornell game. He walked through the train, stopped in the bar car for three Heinekens, and continued down almost to the end, where he threw his stuff in the seat on the aisle. He opened one of the beers and settled in next to the window.

John took the short trip to Philadelphia enough to know all the places and all their names. During breaks from college and business school he had ridden trains across Europe and even into Russia, the first in his family to go anywhere like that. But he didn't enjoy not knowing where he was. Rather, this trip was *his* train ride, the ride home. It afforded him just enough time to get mentally prepared. He liked putting his face against the cold window as the train made its way south through the industrial wasteland stations at Newark and Metropark, to more habitable ground of New Brunswick and Princeton Station, through Trenton and on to places like Cornwall Heights, before slowing down into Philadelphia.

When his mother died, John was the only one who recovered. And he knew he would be the same way now that Mike was gone. He had learned to rely on himself. "Yep," he said out loud, his inner thoughts forcing through. Mike had given in to colon cancer the previous afternoon. It was hard to believe he was dead.

by our heavenly Father to protect us against the supreme
enemy Satan and all of the fallen angels. As with the
archangel, our Michael Donegan often saw it as his duty
to protect us. Michael took wounds in the service of the
Lord, Jesus Christ. Always on the lookout for evil that
might face us, whether by serving in the armed forces or
loving his family in the manner in which he did, as we
all remember the bond between Michael Christopher and
his mother, our dear Rosemary, God bless her beautiful
soul. Though Michael had many shortcomings and was
a sinner like the rest of the holy children of the Father,
he was in his soul a protector of Christ, an archangel in
the spirit of his namesake, Saint Michael. Today he comes
back into the heart of Jesus Christ and rejoins the Holy
Spirit. He is returning to the house of the Lord. Let us
read from the Gospel of Saint Mark…"

When the service was over, John went to find
Bobby Murray, whom he saw sitting alone in the back.
He found him outside the church, smiling and chatting
with a few people. He was a big guy, a lot heavier than
John remembered. He was the only black person at the
funeral, a well-known regular at the same bars as Mike.
Last John knew, he was in the union at Boeing.

"Bobby, hey man," John said.

"Hey, Jack." The two hugged. "Long time. Sorry
about Mike, man."

"Thanks, thanks. Hey, seriously, thanks for coming."

"Aw, c'mon," said Bobby. "Let me tell you
something. Mike was a friend of mine. Me and him went
way back. Way back. He was a stone-cold dude, but he
was a *warrior*, you know what I mean? He was a good
guy, your brother. God bless him."

"Will you come over the house for a while?"

"I'm gonna try to stop by. I gotta go to work, you know. It's busy as hell down there. I'll try. Hey, where's Donny?"

"Back there with my dad," said John.

"All right," Bobby said. He shook John's hand and headed toward the church. "I might see you later."

5.

John's old friends, Kenny and Maria, drove him to his father's house after the burial. There wasn't enough room in the hearse, and John didn't want Mary Meehan feeling awkward. John preferred to be with his friends for a few minutes before diving back in anyway.

"Ok." Maria had printed out a list of the most popular things from 1978.

Kenny said, "Probably disco."

"That's right," said Maria. "'Stayin' Alive.' Bee Gees."

"Perfect," said John.

John and Kenny were best friends since being assigned the same locker at Indian Lane Junior High School. John had been in New York City for the past fifteen years, and they didn't see each other much. Ken was an offensive lineman in high school who got a CPA and became an accountant for a mobile-phone start-up. Maria, always the smartest, had a law degree and did real estate part time as she raised the kids. Kenny and Maria were a couple since tenth grade, and John was the third wheel. John had a few girlfriends float in and out, but mainly it had been the three of them.

As he looked at Maria from the backseat, John thought about how different she was from his sisters. She was a bright, brutally articulate girl from an educated, if still poor, Italian family. Her father taught art history at the community college, and her mother, Angela, was an Italian immigrant thrust into the role of American housewife. Angela Ursotti and Maria went to Mass together constantly, even through high school, when most girls avoided their mothers. It was the one true thing Maria shared with her mother, and while she did it out of duty and loyalty, she also developed faith. Maria loved Flannery O'Connor and Thomas Aquinas and had no problem telling lawyers' kids from the sprawling neighborhoods of Upper Providence with more secular, agnostic tastes that they were morons.

"Let's see, what else?" said Maria. She read through the list. "Pete Rose, three thousandth hit...Pope John Paul I dies, John Paul II takes over...*Darkness on the Edge of Town* released."

"Wow. *Darkness*," said John.

"*Badlands*," said Kenny.

"*Promised Land*," said Maria. "Who won the World Series?"

"Yankees," said Kenny.

"I hate the Yankees," said John. And then, after a second, "Mike hated the Yankees."

"Me, too," said Kenny, eyes on the road.

"Me, too," said Maria. "Fuck the Yankees."

6.

Whenever John returned to Pennsylvania, the first thing that grabbed his attention was the smoke. Cigarettes blended with the smell of the fireplaces burning all over their block. The surfaces in the house had not been redone in twenty or maybe thirty years, and the yellows had gone brown and the greens a dull gray. The house seemed smaller each time he returned, more decrepit, more Catholic. Christ was everywhere, as were the faded mass cards with inscriptions like *In Memory of Margaret Dugan* or *Walter Coughlin—Blessed Be Thy Soul* over watercolor pictures of Jesus with a golden tunic, chestnut beard and hair, and those blue, blue eyes. And today there was a new one that read *Forever in our hearts, Michael Christopher Donegan Jr.*, with the blessed Virgin Mary in a blue frock with a tilted head and beams of light shooting out of her hands.

John was greeted with slaps of hello all around from cousins, neighbors, and nephews, and his face was held with both hands by aunts who kissed him. The group stood in the living room drinking and smoking, but they were pretty quiet. Father Walsh hadn't even left the reception yet. It was the stage before the shine hits: the ties were still on, and the shirts yet unstained with sweat. John whispered to Kenny, "Watch out for this crowd when it gets loose." It was half past five. The men had thick necks and jowls and mustaches, and almost every one of them was in his only suit, polyester with pleats in the pants bought on sale at Penney's or Boscov's. The women, as Donny said, came in two flavors: black-haired with fine and pretty features ("the ones you screw") and sweet-natured with fat ankles and fat asses ("the ones you marry"). John always wondered if it had occurred to Donny that his descriptions fit their own sisters.

The bar in the kitchen had two-liter bottles of Jameson, Canadian Club, Seagram's Seven, Gilbey's Gin, Smirnoff Red Label Vodka, and cans of tonic water, 7UP, club soda, and ginger ale. There was an aluminum tub stocked with ice and lots of Miller Lite and Budweiser. There were two-gallon cartons of red and white wine. The only food for the fifty or so mourners in the house was a large platter of lunch meat: turkey, ham, and roast beef with tomatoes, green and black olives, and a plastic tub of mayonnaise next to some soft round rolls. Aunt Marian brought a small plate of deviled eggs and slices of Lebanon bologna stuffed with cream cheese.

"There are no wakes in America," John said, talking to himself for the third time that day. It was just what happened after a funeral in their small corner of the world. It was a bastardized tribal ritual, no more a proper Irish wake than a sports bar in Parkside was a pub in Dublin.

Mary Meehan came through the crowd to grab John. "Jackie, there you are. Come. Let me get you a drink, love. Your father is in the kitchen."

"Mary, you remember Kenny and Maria," said John.

"Of course. Hello, you two." She gave them kisses.

Mary Meehan was not slowed down by a funeral. In her late sixties, she was in fine form, a handsome woman with a shock of white hair and not-so-bad gin blossoms at the cheekbones. She had become Mickey's companion thirty years ago after a coincidence of cancer took her husband, too. They married once a respectful amount of time passed, but inside the family she was still called "Mary Meehan," because no one wanted to trounce on the graves. She wasn't John's mom, not by a long stretch, but she filled in and took care of his dad, and for that he was grateful.

As they came through the crowd, Mickey was telling stories, going in and out of an Irish brogue: "You know what my mother—she was from the old country—you know what she said when Mike was born? She came to me in the hospital and said, 'Ah…best to name him Michael, Mick. It's a good name…That's why I give it to you…The fishermen say, "Plenty comes to the boat on Michaels' Day…"'" Mickey saw John. "Hey, there's my boy. And, my God, Kenny…and Maria."

"Mick-ey," said Kenny. And he grabbed Mickey's shoulders, pulled back, looked him in the eye, and said softly, "We just want to say sorry about Mike. I know he's in a better place." Maria moved in to give Mickey a hug.

"It's all right, it's all right," Mickey said gently as he hugged Maria back and looked at Kenny and John. His tie was loosened, and his white shirt was rolled up, revealing his forearms, broad and strong from years of hard work. Deep within the aging and liver-spotted skin was the faded ink of a World War II tattoo, the kind you knew was the product of a one-night leave in Boston or Baltimore or San Diego. Mary Meehan once told John that Mickey confided that he wished he could remove it. "I didn't join the goddamn marines or anything," he said. "I was just a guy from Scranton who got drafted into the navy, like everybody in those days. We were all scared as hell."

Mickey took John's elbow and said, "Jackie, come here. I want to show you something." They walked to Mickey and Mary's bedroom on the third floor. When they were alone, Mickey produced a money clip and handed it to John.

"This is Mike's. I thought you should have it."

John looked at the silver clip and its contents: no cash, but there were school pictures of Margarita and Ava from three or four years earlier and a picture of Mike and Ava in front of a roller coaster at Great Adventure.

There were two credit cards: a PNC bank card and a card that denoted membership in some form of discount club at McAleer's Taproom on Baltimore Pike.

Then John saw a little torn piece of notebook paper with Mike's handwriting that read *BVM Novena: Day 1, Mom. Day 2, Ava. Day 3, Margarita. Day 4, Joanie. Day 5, Debbie. Day 6, Annemarie. Day 7, Margie. Day 8, Mary M., Day 9, Holy Mother.*

7.

Eventually, the kitchen thinned out, and a group was left sitting around the maple dinner table. The kids who had been there—strangled by ties, bored, and confused—were now in front of a TV somewhere or long gone. Ashtrays and empty beer bottles littered the table. The guys drank shots of Jameson. Besides John, Kenny, and Maria, there was a smattering of Donegan cousins and Donegan friends from the neighborhood— Mike's friends, people he had known all his life. The stories were starting.

"Who was that girl from Indian Lane who was *so* in love with him?" said Margie.

"Shannon Kelly," said Annemarie. "The skinny one from Nether Providence. She moved away—she married a guy in New York."

"Michael was so good looking when he was young," said one of the women.

"The thing I will never forget," said Donny, "was that he didn't complain about his teeth. I mean, when we were in high school, Mike's teeth were black in the back. He never said a word about it. I think he finally saw a dentist in the army."

Kevin Morris

Carmen D'Ignazio said, "Yo, ok. I got a story about your brother—you wanna hear a story about your brother?" Carmen was younger than Mike but had been around Donny and Annemarie and Margie his whole life. He left school when he was seventeen to work at his father's auto body shop. He had a mustache and was a pain in the ass, but he would come over in the middle of the night to replace an old lady's blown fuse. Carmen was a fact of life for the Donegans, like the woods off of Middletown Road or the trolley running from Media to Sixty-Ninth Street.

"Go ahead, Carm," said Annemarie.

"I was about fifteen. Mike was five or six years older than us, and we thought he was, like, some scary dude who was Donny's brother. It was, like, seventy-three, seventy-four maybe. People don't remember, but it was nuts back then. The country was crazy. Nixon, all that crap. Lots of shit, lots of racial shit. Anyway, I'll never forget it; we were out at the Dairy Queen that used to be down on Pennell Road near Brookhaven, in front of the Kmart. I was with Jimmy Mingey."

"Oh shit," said Donny, "Jimmy Mingey. Je-sus Chriiiist."

They recognized the name, the face, and the reputation of not just Jimmy Mingey but all the Mingeys, a family of nine children, with everyone remembering the Mingey that they knew best. Some recalled affairs; some recalled football practice; some recalled playing pinball at the mall in junior high. But everyone at the table, young and old, knew a Mingey, had a Mingey story, and because they had all lived with them all their lives, knew that Carmen's story would profit from having a Mingey in it. Backs of chairs were pulled closer to the table.

"So, me and Mingey, we smoked and smoked and smoked on this one day until we were stupid, right? We were fuck upped as a nigger's checkbook." He took a drag of his cigarette. "So we decide to walk to the Dairy Queen and get ice cream cones. Back then there was nothing to do except get stoned and go to the Dairy Queen."

Nods all around. "Hey, it's still what I do," said Peter. Margie laughed, which made her start to cough, for which she slapped Peter in the arm.

"So, me and Mingey are getting ice cream cones, and there's this black girl there in line with us. She orders a strawberry sundae — I'll never forget it — a strawberry sundae. And Mingey — the dumbass — goes, 'I like berries,' or something like that. The black girl looks him up and down and goes, 'Fuck you. Ain't nobody *aks* you what you like.'"

There were smiles all around the table. They loved it. John and Kenny both looked at Maria, who was no fan of Carmen D'Ignazio. She was smiling, going with the flow for this one.

"Now, I'm ignoring it," Carmen said. "I start walking back to the road or whatever. Then out of the corner of my ear, I hear Mingey mumble something to her. So I just keep on walking and say, 'Let's go, Minge.' I'm just heading to the parking lot...da da da, you know, all stoned and happy...Next fucking thing you know, four big niggers get out of a Cutlass and start heading at Mingey. Big bucks, big, gigantic niggers with Afros." Carmen put his hands six inches from each side of his side of his head to indicate the size.

Eyebrows raised, mouths opened up, and everyone grinned. John checked Maria again.

"So Mingey backs up. They had those solid stone picnic tables, remember?

"Solid stone, yup," said Peter.

"Right? You remember, Pete? So we back up behind them tables, and I'm looking for anything, like a broken beer bottle, piece of glass, anything. And I'm thinking, 'Oh God, this is it. I'm gonna die here today at the fucking Dairy Queen!'" He took a drag on his cigarette. "One of the niggers comes up to Mingey and says, 'What did you say to my sister?' and he pushes Mingey in the chest. Then he goes, 'With all that mouth, you must like to get your ass kicked.'" Carmen looked around, savoring the moment. "But then he stops like he's just going to scare Mingey and not do anything else. So, we're standing there—and remember, we're all fucked up, and to top it off, Mingey is *crazy*, right?" Carmen was laughing to himself now. "So, Mingey stares right at him and goes...'Fuck you.'"

The table erupted. Beer bottles and shot glasses were slammed down. The drunkest ones laughed loudest, but even the most sober grinned hard.

"So, now they're mad. I don't know whether to run or what...and then—I swear on my mother's life—there's this huge screech in the parking lot. Right out of a movie. And this navy-blue Grand Torino comes flying up. The door opens, and we all look over—even the niggers—and...it's like time stopped. Here comes Mike. I don't know how or where he came from—even to this day—but he just comes flying out of the car. He's got an army jacket on and that wild long hair and beard.

And he's got a two-foot Stillson pipe wrench in his hand, and it's, like, gold—he had a gold Stillson pipe wrench. Who knows where the hell he ever got that? Never seen one before or since. He points it at the big nigger in the front, and he goes, 'Whoa, whoa, whoa, back up, back up!' And the nigger just freezes. I couldn't believe it. He just stands there looking at Mike."

"Mike let his hair grow when he got back from the service—remember that?" said Annemarie.

"Now, of course," Carmen said, "Mike could talk to niggers. He wasn't afraid of them. And they were kinda scared of *him*, actually. Because he didn't act scared around them."

"Well, he *knew* them," said Peter. "He used to drink down in those bars in Chester. He'd stay down there all day and night. He *lived* with them, for Christ's sake."

John took a cigarette from Donny. Carmen let the crowd settle down.

"So, the main nigger goes, 'What you want, you Billy Jack mothafucka?' And Mike breaks into this crazy smile and says, 'Ok. You want to get it on? Huh? Where you live, anyway? Where you stay? Twenty-First Street? Chester Park? I probably know your brother. I know all you little punk niggers. You want to fight me? I've been to Vietnam, you black motherfucker. I'll kick your ass.' And they stand there for a while looking tough, and Mike just stares at them...*stares at 'em.* I was so fucking scared." Carmen went for the full effect. "Finally, after like three minutes, Mike says to me and Mingey, 'Get in the car.'"

The group was in suspense, waiting. Carmen stood, in full command.

"And then Mike says, 'Mingey, gimme the five in my glove box. I want to get a Dilly Bar.'"

Shrieks of laughter. But Carmen held his arms out.

"Wait, wait…" Carmen said. "Then Mike goes to me and Mingey. 'What do you guys want?'"

Somebody whooped. "*No!*" said Annemarie, above the rest.

Carmen was yelling to be heard. His face was so red it was turning purple. "And then Mike looks at the big black guy and goes, 'How about you? You want something?'"

Margie's eyes sprouted tears. Donny fell halfway out of his chair. John, who had been trying to resist, felt the laughter thunder out of him like air from a tire. His ears rang.

"And the guy goes, 'Nah, man.'" Carmen was crying and laughing and yelling. "And Mike says, 'C'mon, get something.'"

"So the black guy thinks about it, and then he says, 'Let me get a chocolate cone.'" Carmen gasped for air between words. "And…Mike…says, 'Like, chocolate *ice cream*…or the chocolate *shell*? Which one?'"

Peter fell into Donny's lap. Carmen was bent over, veins popped out of his neck and forehead standing in front of the table. The words sputtered out.

"And…the…guy…goes, 'Chocolate *ice cream*, man…You're crazy, you know that?' And then he laughed at Mike and shook his head. And that was it."

The group at the table stomped and clapped. As they recovered, they reached for cigarettes and grabbed beers. After a minute, Peter shook his head and backhanded tears from his eyes. "That was Mike."

8.

John and Maria walked to the driveway and lit up Marlboro Lights bummed from Donny.

"Look at this place," said John.

"Never changes," said Maria.

"Thanks for coming. I know it's tough."

"Oh please. Knock it off. What? Because I might hear Carmen or some other guy say 'nigger'? I grew up with these guys, too."

"Where's Kenny?"

"He's talking to Donny and all Mike's friends. He sees those guys all the time. He had Carmen and Peter do our bathroom."

They were sitting on the bumper of a pickup truck. "Can you believe they still smoke like that?" said John. "He died of lung cancer. *Lung cancer.*"

"We're smoking."

"True." He looked at Maria. He could tell she had something on her mind. "What?" he said. "What is it?"

"Judge not least thee be judged, John."

"C'mon."

"No, seriously. Sure, I sit there and think, 'Carmen D'Ignazio, ugh. "Nigger" this, "nigger" that. Since third grade—always been like that. These guys are pigs. Nothing around here will ever change.' But then I think, 'Who am I kidding?' I don't know. Who's so different? I don't get on a fucking elevator in a parking lot if I have to ride alone with a black guy. Where's that leave *me*?"

"Yeah, but that's different."

"Oh yeah? How? How is that different?"

"Do I really have to explain the difference between you and Carmen?"

"No. I'm talking about the difference between *you* and Carmen," said Maria. "And *you* and Mike. And *you* and everybody."

The became silent. After a while he said, "You know what I say? I say, 'Here's to Mike.'"

"Ok. Here's to Mike," she said. They clinked her plastic wine cup against his Budweiser.

"I'm glad he gave up. I'm glad it's over. He was miserable."

"Don't say that."

"C'mon. We've been talking about this all our lives. The entire circus with the candles and the martyrs and the prophets. All that crap. And then I have to listen the priest say Mike was a 'fighter for the Lord, an archangel to protect us all from Satan.' What horseshit."

"He's a priest, jackass. Of course that's what he said."

"Oh really?" Something went off in John. "No, Maria." His voice cracked. "Don't you tell me that. Mike did not win any battle against evil. He was my big brother. When he was a kid, girls loved him, and boys wanted to *be* him. Old men got up on Saturday morning and went out in the snow to see him play basketball in gyms with no bathrooms. When people saw him play, they thought he would be the president. And you know what happened? He got drafted. And then our mom died. No matter how many novenas she said or we said, she died. And my brother went downhill from then on. He was part of a grim fucking mathematical fucking universe."

"Ok, calm down," she said.

"He came back, and we were scared of him." He started to cry. "He smoked pot and took reds and whites and went to bars and came home and slept in his army jacket. He ended up in a trailer park in Florida, Maria. That's what happened. He would call me collect for money for the doctor for his baby. He got in a fight in a bar in Jersey and broke a guy's jaw so bad they sued him. And then he gets cancer like my mother, and where is he now? He is dead. Just like we will all be. Dead. He didn't protect us from anything. He is not a good story. He's a sad fucking story. I don't care about Vietnam; it's not about that. It was good, it was bad, who knows… that's for other people to decide. I don't care. I don't give a fuck. I just know he came back and Mom was dead and he was all fucked up. He had two kids who he couldn't pay child support for and aren't even here today to say good-bye." He was yelling at her. "'*He's a priest.*' Don't tell me that."

"Ok," she said, "ok."

"Look at this bullshit," he said. He pulled the piece of notebook paper with nine names from his wallet. "He was saying novenas just like my mother. Pathetic."

Maria looked at it. "Aw," she said. "It's all his girls."

9.

Mary Meehan poked her head out the door and found them. "You guys come talk to me," she said. "Maria, I haven't seen you in forever. Get a drink and come sit down."

They found a place on the sofa and set their drinks on the coffee table atop coasters with the Donegan coat of arms, something Annemarie had brought back from her honeymoon to Ireland.

John picked up one of the mass cards for Mike that were sitting on the coffee table. He felt drained. "Mike would have liked the laser beams. Did he design this with you?" He looked at Maria. "Mike and Mary hung out a lot the last few years, especially after he got sick."

"It's true," said Mary. "He even started coming to Mass with me a couple years ago. He didn't want anybody to know, really."

"I guess that's pretty common," said Maria. "I mean, when you get sick."

"What, when you know you're going to die soon?" John said. Immediately he felt bad. He was getting too drunk. He tried to lighten up. "Maybe. But when I was little, they could never get him to go to church. He said he couldn't take it."

"How's your mother, Mrs. Meehan?" said Maria.

"She's fine, hon," said Mary, but she wouldn't be blown off track. She pointed at John. "You know, Jackie, I want you to know something. Michael changed in the end. I don't know how much any of you kids saw it or how much he'd let you see."

"Well, I tried to talk to him a couple times a week," said John. "But he went spacey on me. I assumed it was the meds, you know, and the chemo. That's what I told myself, at least."

Mary sensed John's guilt and looked into his eyes. "Oh, honey, your brother loved you so much. He was so proud of you." She touched his knee.

"What did you guys talk about toward the end?" John said. "How was he, really?"

"Well, don't take this the wrong way, but we talked about going slow." Then she looked at Maria. "The thing is, Rosemary, your mother, Jackie, God rest her soul— you know she was my friend—anyway, she was always so active. 'Say a Hail Mary' or 'light a candle for this one and for that one' or 'for the earthquake in Timbuktu' or whatever. Saying the Rosary and the novenas. Now, you have to understand, I got over that a long time ago. I haven't said the goddamn Rosary in twenty-five years." She took a sip of wine and thought for a moment. "I just try to let things go. And I think Mike liked that — you know what I mean? I think he related to it."

"Sure," said John.

"But that brings me to the interesting part. I want you to hear this story," said Mary. "It started when the pope died. You know, the one who passed away, Pope John Paul II, the famous one, the one that Arab tried to kill." Maria smiled. "Well, we were watching the funeral right here on this couch; Michael had stopped by — he was already sick — and he sat with me."

"You're kidding," said John. "Mike watched that?"

"So did I," said Maria. "I watched it with my mom."

"Michael sat right here with me," Mary continued, "and the cardinal was giving the eulogy. It was a huge ceremony — so many colors. It was lovely."

"It *was* beautiful," said Maria. "I remember."

"And there was a wonderful part of the eulogy about the old pope losing his own mother at a very young age. And they said what he did was transfer his sadness and loss to love to the Virgin Mary. And *that* sustained him for the rest of his life. That giving over of himself to something beyond is what opened his channel to such deep faith."

"That's right," said Maria.

"I really think Mike changed at that moment," said Mary Meehan. "I felt it. And from then on, it was like he was hooked."

Maria smiled. John said nothing.

"And I will never forget being at Mass a few weeks later. I look next to me, you know, out to the side, quieting myself down the way you do before the priest comes out." She paused, and waived to indicate her left side. Then she let out a laugh. "Here comes Mike, down the aisle. He sits right next to me in the pew. He says, 'Mary, tell me when to kneel. I think I remember everything else.'" She laughed to herself, lost in the memory and the wine.

The three sat on the couch for a while without speaking.

Mary opened her pocketbook and pulled out a little laminated card. "I cut the pope's eulogy out of the newspaper and gave it to Mike. He cut out this section with an exacto knife and had this card made, and he kept it with him. He gave it to me in the hospital before he passed. Here, read it."

John looked at it and read, "*He, who at an early age had lost his own mother, loved his divine mother all the more. He heard the words of the crucified Lord as addressed personally to him: "Behold your Mother." And so he did as the beloved disciple did: he took her into his own home.*'"

After finishing, John said, "At the end, there's some Latin: *Totus Tuus.*"

"Now here's the best part," said Mary. "About six months ago, Mike shows me, right here"—she lifted up her forearm and turned it inward—"he's got a tattoo. And it says: *Totus Tuus.* Big green letters, you know…a tattoo like your father's, like all the kids get these days. You couldn't see it at the viewing because the undertaker dressed him. But it's there. *Totus Tuus.*"

Maria was looking at her hands. After a minute, without lifting her head, she said, *"Totally yours."*

"That's right," said Mary, nodding. *"Totally yours."*

John got up to look for Donnie to bum another smoke. As he moved toward the center of the house, where the crowd was dying down, he wished for a cold, cold night from long ago, when basketball was holy and he could sleep in Annemarie's bed.

Mulligan's Travels

Jim Mulligan stood in boxers and a T-shirt in the refrigerator light, beer bottle in hand, in the same spot as countless American men before and since, at once living the whiteness and watching it, a picture within a picture, hoping for a miracle snack. He was somewhat medicated, overtired, and experiencing the conflation of his three more or less permanent worries: work, money, and what to eat. Nothing moved him.

Mulligan had learned to accept such times of doubt and pain, but at the moment he was caught up in something else, something careless he had done. When he had walked into his house in Brentwood two hours before at midnight, he realized he had left a brand-new shirt in the hotel room in New York. The lapse ate at him. He loved that goddamned thing, with its small logo of intertwined dollar signs in distressed ink on the back collar. It was roomy and chocolate colored and made from thermal underwear material, a cool shirt from a cool store, the kind of effortlessly hip clothing it was so hard to find. At fifty, with an undefeatable gut, he faced the attendant problem of finding clothes that struck the right balance between young and old, thick and thin.

It was not supposed to be this way. This was not supposed to be his life. He had started for the UCLA football team for three seasons, and his self-image was still that of a free safety, lean and stalking, ready to pounce. He could change the game by making plays. Now he just watched and obsessed along with any other fan, gradually losing his battle to stay fit, which meant losing the battle to stay sharp and distinct, which meant wending his way to old age and dying.

Tight shirts from Maxfield and Fred Segal were ridiculous. Sports jerseys didn't work anymore. Everything was a brand from a chain bought in a mall. His solution was devolving, the way the solution to a bad day was getting drunk. Any time he was not in a suit, he reached for the same things: the same jeans, the same blank XL dark-blue T-shirt, the same sneakers. The new brown shirt had represented a welcome opportunity to revive his vanishing style. It was nondescript enough to satisfy his dislike for clothing that shouted its brand name, branded enough not to be plain, and comfortable enough that he didn't feel like a sausage in its casing. It was miraculously lightweight, wearable without a jacket in the fall in Los Angeles. It was a step in the right direction. It showed he wasn't giving in.

He went to the bed where Rita was sleeping with their daughter, Isabella, and their snoring English bulldog, Henry. There was no room for three humans plus Henry, so he carried the big, dumb, lovable, brown-and-white-brindled dog into Bella's room. The task was growing increasingly difficult. When Mulligan returned and climbed under the covers, he noticed that, even after extracting old ninety-pound King Henry, neither wife nor daughter woke up. He wished one of the girls had at least opened an eye, asked, *God, what time is it?* and, comforted by his arrival, had fallen back to sleep. They didn't stir, leaving him in his own company, to return to his troubles.

Again with the shirt. It had been a birthday present from their longtime housekeeper, Mariana, of all people, and he thought back to how Bella had said "*aww*" when he opened it. He had been nonplussed and skeptical of how it would look, only noting later—and only to himself—that it was kind of great.

He checked his BlackBerry for new messages— he was expecting messages. Finding none, he plugged the device into its charger and set it on top of his iPad. The New York trip had not gone well. The MexiCloud deal he had been trying to put together for two years was in danger. The pressure was snowballing: the firm's fee was to be paid when the transaction closed, and his salary had been cut by 25 percent until he got it finished. All his eggs were in the MexiCloud basket— dangerous in light of his big monthly nut. There were six mortgages on four properties: the Brentwood house they had lived in for two years, the Brentwood house they had moved from but not sold because it would not sell, the place in Park City, and the place in the desert. Piled on top were various other obligations: cars, household employees, private schools, charitable pledges, and a troubled closed-end technology fund that had been making unexpected capital calls. Like most of his peers—he knew this because they talked about it— Mulligan calculated his net worth daily. Depending on his mood, the mood of the newspapers, and his mood after gauging the mood of the papers, he was worth somewhere between four and ten million bucks.

The MexiCloud deal, which involved buying ten thousand new automated teller machines and supporting enterprise software and data-storage infrastructure for the Mexico-based operations of his client, HNBC-Bering-Bloodworth, should not have been so complicated. It should have been like calisthenics. Mulligan's career had tracked the rise of the cash machine. He realized very early—it didn't take a rocket scientist—that the ATM was the future of money, and he ascended smoothly through the ranks of his first job at Harriman Hartman as an investment banker (or advisor) for transactions between the manufacturing companies that made ATMs and the commercial banks, otherwise known as "regular" banks, which in the past twenty years had deployed the machines in every branch and on every street corner in America. While Rita quit practicing law and reinvented herself as a mom and private-sector productivity consultant who worked from home, he worked like a fire ant, spending all-nighters with bankers from Drexel and missing Bella's fall graduations and most softball games. He earned promotions, played golf, had season tickets, went to lunch, went to Vegas, went to New York, went to Hawaii, and got Bella into Harvard-Westlake.

On the run up in the nineties and into the new century, Mulligan's ATM niche was a way to make easy money from the public's desire for easy money. He and his LA-based team became the go-to bankers for integrating new third-party data-storage methods, beginning with server farms and then, in recent years, leading the charge into the use of cloud computing to handle the infinite on-the-spot daily transactions. Mulligan specialized in keeping it simple: he had no clue how the millions of little machines he placed kept track of the bazillions of dollars that blazed around each day, but he did know how to put together all the people who made all of the stuff, and he had faith that he could conceive of and deliver the most profitable strategies. He pioneered debt-financed purchasing, the use of sale-leasebacks, Bahamian joint ventures, and the issuance of special securities to maximize the value of ATMs. This made him, he explained to Bella when she asked, an investment banker for companies, and sometimes those companies were banks. So, yes, he told her, you could call him a banker for banks. This became more complicated, of course, once Citibank, which everyone called simply "the Bank," bought Hartman Harriman. Thereafter, he became a banker for banks inside the Bank, until his division got spun off in the wake of Lehman—which he called "the Mess"—creating the new yet old-sounding firm Harriman Hartman Citi, at which point Mulligan returned to being a plain old banker for banks.

Now the boom was over, and everyone lived in post-Mess times. It was harder to hit the numbers so easily yielded in years gone by, and there was less room to be creative and less of the casino feeling of endless opportunity. Congress was closing in on the bullshit fees banks could charge consumers for the privilege of rubbing the ATM genie. Harriman's banking bankers, of whom he was in charge, looked abroad for a second chance, which meant looking south, for the easy money, or so they thought. Having taken what turned out to be the anfractuous assignment of Latin America, he was trying to help a current client (HNBC Bering-Bloodworth) leapfrog the current generation of ATMs in Mexico, almost every one of which he had helped place five years earlier in a killer deal he had middled on behalf of a former client (Banco Popular de Oaxaca), the *current* leader, which, through its *current* investment bank, Mulligan's biggest competitor, argued that in these uncertain times—with the coming of the cloud, in other words—all that was needed was an upgrade of the *former* deal, an argument that could potentially scotch the *current* deal, which he needed desperately in order to remain among the very rich and not just the rich, which required, according to *Barron's*, a person to have ten million bucks.

Mulligan interlaced his fingers and hit his ducked forehead three times quickly: he had sworn he would never get in this spot, that he would never be one of the guys about whom other guys said, *That's too bad; he just kind of blew it.* He had been one of the smart ones, nowhere near the wreckage of the Mess. If anything, as Bob Rubin said on more than one conference call, guys like Jim Mulligan saved the day because it was the *regular* banks with the deposits—which were only bolstered by the easy money at the ATM—that possessed the balance sheets strong enough to pull all the other idiots through the Mess. Jim Mulligan had been one of the ones doing the clucking as the Masters of the Universe scrambled to save their asses. If it had not been for the people like him outside New York, plying away in the provinces, assisting the boring old regular banking business, and staying out of the ridiculous derivatives and CDO swaps, the whole ship could have gone down. But now, just a few years later, here he was in trouble, trying to squeeze margin out of impossible new markets, debts rising, salary decreasing, nuts in a wringer, while the pricks who caused the Mess were making money again.

Sleep did not come, so he grabbed the iPad, which sat on his bureau glowing in the dark. He still didn't have any new e-mail, but the always-encouraging moving circle went round at the bottom. It said, *Searching...* and he hit his favorite app, Check Mate! trying not to think about the lost shirt or the almost-lost deal. Instead he wondered whether the app came through the Internet and thus would not now show up because the Wi-Fi wasn't working due to spotty reception in the bedroom, or whether, since Check Mate! had been downloaded, it was always there, permanently embedded on the hard drive or — he guessed that this was the way they did it now — the device's virtual replica of the hard drive in the cloud. It was one of those moments of technological helplessness that weaved in and out of his life, like not knowing when an attachment would open on a BlackBerry or, during his brief flirtation with a MacBook, how he could get on the Internet without knowing the answer to that old Mac question of whether his Ethernet connection was via a DCPH1 or ANDN protocol.

Then lo, his unfinished game from the plane filled the screen. Crazy as it was given the nature of his job, Mulligan didn't understand much of what made any of these things work. Truth was he was a salesman: salesmen sell, and the best salesmen in the world traveled around the business of money. He could have just as well sold shovels, and he would have happily put together Bahamian joint ventures for shovel companies if shovels were in the right place at the right time, like ATMs. Secretly he was clueless most of the time about the fundamentals of connectivity and information technology. He wondered if his weakness was related to his lifelong lack of knack for the everyday. He could not fix anything — couldn't change a tire, couldn't hang a picture, and could barely replace batteries. Still, just because he wasn't handy by nature didn't mean he had to be digitally dumb. Logic would dictate that he should be better with technology because he was numbers oriented — after heading west to play football, he went to Stanford Business School, where he focused on finance and did well enough to land an impressive job at Harriman in LA, which, in fine Mulligan form, he started right after graduation. As a result, by now he knew just about everything he needed about the intricacies of banking and investments. Shouldn't a more educated type understand techy stuff better than a tradesman? It wasn't the same as mechanical, all this computer crap. Or was it? Maybe he was wrong. Maybe not knowing if an attachment would open was *exactly* the same shortcoming as not having a clue as to how to change a fuse or fix a hot-water heater.

When practical problems arose throughout his life, he paid people to fix things, just as he had promised his brother, Dennis, when they were teenagers, upon being challenged as to exactly what the fuck he was going to do when the electricity went out in his house or when one of his kids needed a Pinewood Derby car: *Simple. I'm going to pay some guy to do it for me.* It may have been forgivable that he said such a thing, because of their station in life then, when he and his brother were using his mother's portion of his father's support payment of food stamps to buy dinner in an exurb of Hartford. It certainly did not seem likely when that now-famous line was spoken that either of them would one day be paying anyone to do anything. But Mulligan managed to climb out through football and hard work in school and the desire not to worry about money ever again. He figured out quickly that the poor were poor because they didn't acquire anything. So, as his salary grew, he concentrated on accumulating assets at all turns, buying stocks, municipal bonds, and—perhaps foolishly—the real estate upon which the mortgages currently eating him had been taken.

The problem these days was not all the new technology. New technology in and of itself was great. He had made a fortune from it. Nor was the problem too much technology. The pundits who opined about the negative effects of information overload, of overconnectedness and too much choice, of a society being entertained and digitized to death, did not have it quite right. The thing that was killing people — the *problem*—was that the *shit did not work. Nothing ever worked.* He popped himself in the head with his interlaced fingers again. There was human error, sure. He was the first to admit that he himself sometimes did not, in fact, know how to execute things. But, more often, it was the product that did not do its job. The ability to get money out of a machine or watch a 1977 Creedence Clearwater Revival video anytime and anywhere or get into the movie theater with a piece of paper you printed at home was great. But once the possibility of getting cash or watching a Creedence video or getting into the movies with a plain old dipshit piece of paper existed, an *expectation* was created. The monster was out of the box. And one did not need to be the Unabomber to see that the monster did not always show up when needed. *That* was the problem. People ended up spending most of their time trying to find out when and how the cash machine would give money or whether the video would buffer. People stopped their cars in cul-de-sacs or walked out on the porch to get cell reception or set their laptops by the espresso maker facing the pantry shelves in the kitchen or were told *almost there* while they waited *a few more seconds* for the goddamn basketball game to come on. People wondered why the car phone worked less on foggy days and whether that could *really* be the reason, like whether turning your beach chair to face the sun *really* worked. Everywhere, promised connections were not being made, and the humans who had bought a solution were left trying to solve a problem. People went down depressions into hollows to survive. So much so that the hollows became comfortable — preferable to the constant exposure to mistakes, malfunctions, and unmet expectations. Taken with the diminishing nature of a finite lifetime, choices became more important, multiplying daily, requiring constant double downs of the just-to-break-even variety, until there were no choices left other than to find a hollow.

He rose to go to the bathroom, where he took an Ambien, making it two that night — a no-no, but he had to get to sleep. He picked up the iPad one more time as he lay back down to see if the analyst in New York had redone the numbers. There was still no service. His inbox was unchanged. The last message was still the one from his wife that he had read on the plane. He had missed Bella's fourth-grade class' party, having stayed in the city for one more meeting, and Rita had e-mailed him this:

> It went great. Really cute. She had a ball. They were in the pool most of the time, but it broke into a whiffle-ball game around four...boys v. girls of course. Monica and I both said how fun it was to c the girls all in their little bikinis running around not self-conscious. Probably last time for that – soon there will be body worries. Fly safe. We ate but Mariana left something in there for you. XX

He listened to the girls sleep. Bella was a miniature version of Rita, like the same document zoomed down to 60 percent. He was proud of their shared jokes, their love of dogs and horses and guinea pigs, and their obsession with *Say Yes to the Dress*. And he was lucky for his daughter: Bella worked hard to keep him happy. She was always up for a visit to the office, and when they were alone in the car, she asked about his life. She complained when he went away and told him not to smoke cigars. But lately she could vanish in a cascade of tears from an innocuous conversation. Before he knew it, Rita would be standing hands on hips in the doorway asking him what the hell he'd said, like when Bella admitted to liking a boy and he asked, perfectly harmlessly, if any of her friends were into the same guy. Or when he told her not to worry about being ugly because her braces would

be off soon, thinking they were in the teasing space of
buddies, misjudging that, though Bella often wore the
X chromosome, it was really just to be nice to him and
didn't give him the right to treat her like a golf buddy.
Back at the iPad, he made one wrong move, and the
black queen came roaring across screen. His king was
cornered. He started another game.

———

When Rita and Bell awoke, they did not wake him, or at
least not enough for him to acknowledge consciousness.
He thought he felt Bella kiss his cheek. Rita wrote a
note that he found on the bed stand:

> Went to the Barn. Let Sondra in and ask
> her to please get the cushions on pool
> chairs. meet us for lunch, Bye.

Underneath, Bella's handwriting read:

> *Yo dawg, where you been? LU xo B.*

Mulligan rose and went through his ablutions.
Helpless as to breakfast, he considered going to
Starbucks but remembered his one-man boycott of its
bullshit. The weird thing about the Northwesternization
of the culture was its false patina of hipsterism and
liberal politics: it was all so green, healthy, smug, and
egalitarian. But no one was greedier than the geeky
tech trillionaires up there on stages, endless stages,
walking around like stand-up comedians with concealed
microphones, introducing products to beaming crowds

of devotees in San Jose, Palo Alto, and Redmond—or Cupertino, a name that said it all. How could it all be so fucking great? Weren't eight people killed every day texting while driving? Could he be the only one confused by how the crunchy, organic, artisan, environmentalist, pro-third-world, and anti-child-labor ethos found room to embrace the iPad with 4G? Starbucks sold *coffee*, for God's sake, and widow makers like apple fritters and iced cinnamon rolls. Software programs stole all the world's music. And the parents of every fourth grader did not know what to do in the face of their kid's desire to join Facebook. He longed for a day when *Boeing meant jobs* and it was weird for Seattle to even have a football team.

Mulligan took the iPad and his BlackBerry and went across the lawn, past the pool, to his home office in the guesthouse, where he turned on his desktop. It did not boot up correctly, which he theorized was related to Bella's going on illegal music sites. He had sixteen new e-mails on his BlackBerry but none on his iPad. Fourteen of the sixteen e-mails were from the bank's analyst in New York. Each had important attachments— complicated accounting spreadsheets on special proprietary enterprise software—that were impossible to view on the BlackBerry. That meant, with the iPad not updating due to the Wi-Fi connection issue and the desktop not working at all, Mulligan found himself with three devices turned on and no spreadsheets. He picked up the phone, which was cordless, to dial the bank's twenty-four-hour IT service. After three rings, a two-tone noise preceded a recording: *To complete this call, you must first dial nine...Please hang up and dial again*. He felt sweat over his brow. The voice was *not* telling him that what he had wrong was the usual unknowable difference between dialing one before the area code or not dialing one before the area code. No, he had forgotten to dial nine—nine!—before the number, something which struck him as insane, since it was a call from *home*, and, for the entirety of his professional life, dialing nine had been the exclusive province of the business phone, something you did from the *office*. Dialing nine was something that never—*never*—applied to the home phone. What meant anything if that was not the way it was anymore? The interlaced fingers met forehead once more.

He heard the doorbell—another interruption. It was Sondra, the housekeeper. She was more like an assistant housekeeper who worked on the weekends because Mariana was off. Sondra was illegal, but Mariana had convinced him to hire her on the altogether fair but altogether unspoken premise that Mariana was getting too old to clean the entire house every day. He was (truly) happy to do it, and it made each of the three women— Rita, Bella, and Mariana—happy, which made his life easier. Plus, Sondra was a devout, demure, diminutive, and decorous girl who was thrilled to get four hundred bucks a week, which he paid via personal check because he never had enough cash, even though it was certain to fuck him up one day taxwise. The moral, ethical, and legal ramifications of failing to withhold from someone who was illegal but had a Social Security number and a California driver's license was one of the few mental wormholes of his quotidian life Mulligan had left unexplored. He didn't know what she did about health insurance.

Sondra spoke no English, so he used what Spanish he had garnered from trips to Cabo San Lucas and UEFA Cup games on Univision. This meant he knew only the elementals — for example, that *limpio* meant clean.

"Oh, Sondra, *por favor, necesito limpio*," he said, making a wax-on motion with his hands. "Rita said for me to ask you if you could 'please *limpio*'?"

Sondra nodded vigorously and said, "*Sí, disculpa, pero limpia que? Afuera?*"

He realized she was asking him just exactly what she should clean. Giving in to his inability to communicate in words, Mulligan pointed to the pool chairs. She told him, also in gestures, that first she would walk Henry. He nodded. Before he turned away, she said, "*También, señor, necesito ir a comprar las cosas por casa*," and pantomimed pushing a shopping cart. He remembered that Mariana had delegated the weekly grocery run to Sondra on top of the other grunt work. Mulligan momentarily marveled that he lived in a world where Sondra thought he might be concerned about her workflow plan. He thanked her in Spanish, she thanked him in English, and he beat a retreat back to the technological windmills of the guesthouse.

With all the confusion over attachments, he was late for lunch. The girls wanted him at Rosti on San Vicente at quarter past noon, and he was already more than fifteen minutes late. He closed his eyes in frustration. When would he break through his preoccupation with work? He'd been in New York for a week, hadn't spoken to his wife or daughter in three days, and was a no-show at yet another event that would never come again. It didn't matter that yesterday's party was billed as just another entirely missable school thing; it had turned out to yield a golden moment, a parent's keepsake to be clutched when looking back, when inevitably he would think, *Man, did that go fast*. It was a memory, like so many others, that he would now have to access through the prism of his wife. He looked for his BlackBerry. Not wanting to let the girls down again, he texted Rita: *I'm coming. I will be there. Sorry.*

Mulligan went to his closet and put on the jeans, the blue T, and sneakers. The brown shirt would have been the perfect thing. No response came from Rita, and he knew that meant she was angry, because she — like everyone everywhere — read all texts within five seconds of receipt. In moments like this, no answer from Rita was bad news, her way of leaving him alone to feel rotten about being absent. He raced to the other side of the house and jumped in the car, hitting the button to open the closest of the doors on the four-door garage. His moves combined the precision that comes with having done something a thousand times with the kind of corner cutting you did only when you were in a rush, like not snapping in your seat belt, which he could get to once he backed out of the Kenter Canyon driveway. The car's roof narrowly passed underneath the still-upward-moving garage door. He reached for his sunglasses with his right hand and began rolling the wheel counterclockwise with his left.

Before he could get the glasses to his face, Mulligan heard a muscular and garbled noise, almost like the workings of a trash compactor. He slammed the brakes. The sound had been strange — like something being rolled, very low and dense. He sat silent, hoping the coast was clear. He hoped it might have come from across the street. Maybe the gardeners were mulching something. Or maybe he had run over a branch or Bella's skateboard or something. He shifted back into drive and started forward.

The same low noise shot out, this time punctuated by a higher-pitched yelp. He closed his eyes and lifted his hands off the steering wheel as though it were suddenly ten thousand degrees. He *had* run over something. It was bad—muffled, crunching, and violent. He knew the sound of a body getting hit. He threw open the car door and dove to the ground. There was Henry, wedged under the rear axle, staring at him, a purplish mark on his brindled brow.

Heartbreak slammed into Mulligan's chest. He tried to be calm. "Hey, Henry. Hey, buddy," he said. "C'mon, big boy. Can you come here?" Henry moved his front legs and shoulders, trying to obey, but he got nowhere. Mulligan reached and burned his hand on the exhaust pipe, and when he pulled back in pain, he smashed it against the inside of the wheel housing. He shimmied as far as he could and stretched again but barely touched the hair of the dog's back. He spun over on his back, and tried to reach with his legs but got the same result. He went to the side to try to get at Henry from a different position, but he could only flex his toe thinly against the dog's big shoulders, a pitiful drip of pressure—no match for the crush of the axle.

Sondra was off to the market by now, which left him alone. He felt the sickening rise of panic. He played out the scenes to follow: Henry slowly dying, Sondra crying, Bella shrieking, Rita stunned, and Bella and Rita both staring at him in judgment, forgiving him slowly over years but never, ever, ever forgetting. He stood up and looked for anything—he thought about running next door to the Stanhope's house. He had to do *something.* He dropped down to the ground again. "Hey…Ok, buddy… Hi, boy…You're a good boy…a good king boy…Yeah, that's right. Relax, big boy…" With the next wave of desperation, the defensive back part of his brain took over. He put his shoulder under the bumper and, with a furious groan, tried to lift the car up. It didn't work.

Mulligan came to a knee and tried to collect himself. He thought about hitting the car's OnStar Service button but decided there would not be enough time for whomever they get to come to the rescue to get there. Henry's eyes had that dumb, lovable, low-brain-wave stare, although it was plainly fading. He was crying a little. Mulligan considered dialing 911, but that seemed like it would be even slower than *OnStar.* He jumped to his feet and started running down the driveway to look for help. A few steps later, it hit him: *The jack! Of course! The fucking jack!* Racing to the driver's-side window, he hit the trunk icon, sending the lid on its automated rise. He threw the golf clubs and the rest of the compartment's contents to the side, pulled out the carpeted trunk floor, and began unscrewing the wing nut holding the jack in place. It came out in two pieces, and an instruction sheet was buried below. Mulligan stared at the directions for a few seconds, grasping what he could. He put the stand into the risers and placed the combined unit in front of the right rear tire.

It was then that he realized he was missing the small tool needed to ratchet the thing up. *Where is the fucking crank?* Under the car, Henry struggled and groaned and wore the same heartbreaking stare of confusion. Mulligan peered again at the image of a small elbow-like piece of iron. He tore through a brown paper bag full of hangers and old CDs. Not finding anything, he ripped out the spare tire, hoping the missing crank had fallen into the nether regions of the trunk. He went back to the littered driveway and dumped the contents of his golf bag. Out came his oversize driver, his irons, his putter, half a dozen Titleist twos—which bounced down toward the mailbox—dried-up Cohibas, a cigar cutter, lighters, ball marks, and divot fixers.

He sat on the blacktop amid the array of shit he carried around in his car every day. It was all his fault—twice over. Not only had he run the dog over, he also could not save him. *This is it*, Mulligan said to himself. *This is where I come apart. This is the kind of thing that happens in real life. The bad thing.* He tried to take it in, to taste it like the second week of prison food, like the flesh and the blood. *Sometimes the bad thing happens.* He felt the unwelcome guest of sense memory, a panicky flashback to when three kids from his high school were killed by a drunk driver—the petrified feeling that accompanies abrupt confrontation with a horrible accident. *There is no safety net. Sometimes it is just* all *bad.* He made a decision to settle into the pain and, in this purgatorial time between the lightning bolt and the crack, to sit and watch Henry die.

Then he had an idea. He ran into the garage and pushed a stepladder up against the large wall cabinets. At the top, he found what he was looking for: a red toolbox, barely touched since Christmas five years ago when

Dennis had given it to him as a half joke. The elevated resting place showed how little Mulligan thought of it, and, pulling it down, he was reminded of how heavy it was. He managed himself off the ladder, ran out to the car, and threw the toolbox down—more anxious metal clangs pressed into the silence, more diaspora flowed to the ground. He looked for a set of Allen wrenches, the small tools used to drive hexagonal bolts and screws. He only knew such things existed from a distant but suddenly vivid memory from a high-school class. Having seen that the jack required a hexagonal lever, he got the sense that a large Allen wrench might work on it, and this was what he visualized. He rifled through the toolbox, found the Allen wrenches buttoned up one by one in a clear plastic casing in escalating size, like fifes inside pencil packets. He removed the biggest wrench and dropped to the ground. He inserted the tool and turned it.

He was right—sort of. It fit, but the angle of the jack's opening only allowed him to turn the wrench less than an inch at a time. He had to take it out, adjust, and turn down again, repeatedly, to get any kind of progress. He could not tell if it was taking. *Maybe this is ridiculous*, he thought. But he was out of ideas, so he kept up his attack, cranking the Allen wrench an inch, reinserting it, and then turning it another inch. He felt a wave of failure. *This is not the way it was supposed to work.* His knuckles became raw and then bloody, and his blood mixed with the gravel of the driveway until his fingernails were outlined in black.

He pushed back the panic. "That's a good boy in there, Henry," Mulligan said, continuing to crank frantically but now making eye contact. The bruise on

Henry's face was starting to darken. "I'm getting you out, buddy...getting you out of there. That's a *goot* boy, King Henry. Yes, sir." At the edge of his vision, he sensed a fractional movement—did the lower edge of the Mercedes' chassis rise just a hair? He could not tell for sure, like one could not tell whether it was raining upon feeling a first raindrop. Then it happened again and in definite rhythm with his turning motion. It was working. *It's working.* The jack's interlaced support beams began to extend, like lowercase *x*s becoming capitals. He cranked faster. The car's suspension system lifted and the chassis followed. Beneath the car, Henry became newly calm, and, after a few moments, began to wriggle his front paw with more range. Next, he moved his shoulder, and then half his torso, and then he was out, limping slightly, into the open air of the driveway.

———

Mulligan sat by the pool in a lounge chair. His hands were bandaged, which made it difficult—but not impossible—to hold a cigar. After freeing Henry, Mulligan had carefully put him on his big doggy pillow in the den, made sure that all the doors were shut, and downed a Valium. He showered and waited for the girls, who rushed home from the restaurant to find both Mulligan and Henry bruised and shaken, but ok. A quick trip to the pet clinic verified there was nothing broken. They were lucky, the vet said—a less muscular breed of dog would have died. Rita came out with drinks. Mulligan had a Heineken, and the girls had lemonade from a carton with Paul Newman's picture. Bella lay next to Henry, who lay in his bed snoring.

Mulligan's head swam in a swirl of exhaustion, alcohol, anxiety medication, and nicotine. He felt almost perfect.

"I can't believe I left that shirt back in the hotel," he said.

"Just a shirt," said Bella.

Rita did not look up from her magazine. "I'll go online and find the exact same one."

Bella stroked Henry's neck and cracked a grin. "Yeah, like a do-over."

"Very funny," he said and took a sip of beer.

"I like the shirt you have on now," Bella said, pointing to his tattered UCLA football T-shirt.

"Yeah, I love this one, too," he said, touching its fabric. He considered his cigar and then looked up for the girls. "Tell you what. I'll make dinner."

"Right," Bella said. She rolled onto her stomach and smiled at him, enjoying this. "I wish Mariana heard that."

"Are those braces?" Mulligan said to Bella. "They're very attractive."

She stuck her tongue out at her father. Finding nothing in reach to throw at him, she said,

"Whatever you make would be *so* gross. I *so* wish Mariana was here."

"C'mon. What should I make?"

"Forget it, Mulligan," said Rita. "We ain't taking the bait." She gathered up the glasses and headed for the kitchen. "I'll look at what Sondra bought. I told Mariana to tell her to get steaks." Passing him with her hands full, she bumped the lounge chair with her hip and said, "Relax."

"I am relaxed," he said. "I'm totally relaxed."

"Better to lose your shirt than kill the dog," she said

and then disappeared inside. Bella put her earphones in to listen to music.

"Both of you," he said. "A couple of comedians."

He sat back and felt the sunlight, beer in hand. The MexiCloud attachments remained unopened, and he had not left the house all day. Rita was right about not telling Mariana—Henry's bruise was the sole strand of memory left from the day, and it, like the shock of the moment, was lessening as the hours passed by. The dog slept, Bella drummed her fingers to her song, and Mulligan tried once more to relax.

Rain Come Down

The worst torments the pessimists of the world inflict on its optimists are their instinctual opposition to eating outside on the first mild evening in April; to going with no warning to Atlantic City; letting a snuggly grandchild stow away for the rest of the night; calling for a pizza; voting for Obama; taking a home-equity line to pay for new kitchen cabinets; refusing to honor the nowadays-common custom of ignoring people right there next to you on the plane, saying hi to the nice couple, finding out where they live, how old grandkids are, laughing at the ain't-it-the-truth stuff. Given enough time, the optimists win out, and the pessimists can be found getting into the bumper car; tagging along to the nursing home to visit Aunt Helen; using the MasterCard that's for a rainy day; drinking a Bloody Mary at the tailgate party for the fiftieth high-school reunion (and going in the first place to see all those fat, old people); risking the traffic on 95 into Philadelphia; taking the littlest grandkid out to the pool because she's about to cry; and starting over to the Performing Arts Center even though it's coming down pretty good.

John Collier shut the Volvo door, and for a moment the noise stopped. Like most men who came of age in a less regulated time — in his case, one who rode around in a jeep for two years in Korea — he didn't reach for the seat belt, and the dinging spoiled the silence. Once he buckled, the quiet reigned again, and as the rain fell on the windshield, he felt like he was watching it at the movies, the patter more a sound effect than wet and physical. Imaginative moments like this were more common since he began living with Ann's condition; he wondered if it was how he compensated for the lack of conversation, one of the many adjustments that came with going from partner to caretaker. Collier pulled the car a few yards to the front door, where she stood under the big red and white Titleist umbrella. She turned to ease her too-skinny frame down the Astroturf steps. He made it as quickly as he could around the front of the car and gently helped her in, placing her feet so she sat straight ahead.

Ann smiled as he settled behind the wheel. "Damned if it's not turning to hail," he said. Her teeth were chattering a little, so he turned on the heat, holding his hand up to the air until he was sure it was getting warm. "Ok, then, whadd'ya say, Annie? Let's get on the road." She smiled at him again and faced forward, tugging the tuck of her scarf. To Collier's amazement, with enough time in the morning, Ann could still manage her hair, makeup, and lipstick. She did not know what day it was, yet she maintained the deep patterns of femininity and the pride in her appearance as a beautiful woman. She had chosen the pearls he bought her at Tiffany's in New York many years ago on a weekend trip for their twenty-fifth. "Emily's very excited about this," he said and hit the right turn signal even though he was just going out of the driveway and then out onto the road. "Classical music. You like that, honey. They've brought in a little Japanese girl to play the piano."

———

Today is a special day Annie we are going for a ride. I can't make the breakfast John brings me tea and the waffles from the microwave and the butter and the syrup he puts on for me and Emily called Mom Daddy's going to bring you and hear a concert at the PAC so rainy today honey. John by doorstop red umbrella for golfing brings around the car a safe car much safer these days you can hit a brick wall with that car hon he knows that kind of things I told Nicholas they made gigantic engines where your Pop Pop works in Philadelphia gigantic GE engines for machines worldwide things kids don't think about Emily never did that's for sure. John drives the beat and slide windshield wipers wind shield from strokes of rain against window. Outside all the roads of Middletown I've been riding on these roads in rain all my life they were narrower even some dirt the wind sure does whirl by not too cold getting to be summer we drive Darlington Road mother's house by gravel shoulders of the roads we walked when there were no cars. Look in front look straight at the road my father said don't take your eyes off the road and around John driving talking to me really talking keeping the conversation up everywhere dark green wet trees and gray dry streets now wet and made darker bright yellow from the PENNDOT men paint bright yellow lines with machine rollers these days and the PENNDOT guys so lovely to me always for a stop hello see them talk to them looking up under red emergency helmets and orange raincoats safety was their main concern. More rain sheets of rain beat shields of rain in front see yellowing fields of Jensen's dairy and its 352 where Margie and Bunny died. Oh my these roads that's a long long time ago that '52 Oldsmobile that boy from Haverford whatchamacallit Kretchley or something had that accident when both Margie and Bunny were in it I was their best friend Daddy had to go to the hospital for the body and we cried. John says up this hill and just get over to the left lane here Annie drive and we'll be at the pack that's what Nicholas called it the pack like it was a pack of gum or wolves Nicholas would say when he was much littler. Emily needs to bring him by I have that present for him oh shoot shoot shoot I can't remember a goddamn thing it is still sitting in that closet Chandler's and Megan's too Nicholas is eight Chandler is six Megan is four Emily needs to get me the new school pictures. Dry inside this car—truck—car are you in a truck or a car you're up high like a car. Fresh air little nip in it but nice riding with warm John good John waking me up with breakfast helping me to go and the washing. Feel him there good John not one bit different than I expected between two people for fifty years the radio station oh Annie it's Frank Sinatra you remember this the summer wind can you believe it's the oldies radio songs. It's clearing up that's good Annie.

———

"Hi, Mommy," Emily said as she helped Ann out of the car, ignoring her father. "Don't you look sweet?" She took an inventory of Ann's outfit, making sure there were no disasters. Collier was hovering over the wheel, confused, and Emily realized he didn't know where to park. "Follow the guys with the orange things, Dad. They'll wave you to a spot." She heard his muffled holler through the door and for a moment regretted her decision not to make him stay at home; she sure as hell didn't need whatever instruction he was about to give her. Then she remembered he would need his ticket, which explained his agitation. Emily fished it out of her bag and handed it to him.

She held her mother's arm through the doorway, had their passes scanned, and headed through the lobby, which had the carpeted feel and paneled walls of a well-funded suburban theater. She talked in Ann's ear as they walked. She knew that her mother could hear very little, but the cognitive specialist had told her it couldn't hurt. They flowed with the crowd of locals, their steps syncopating the excitement that precedes all shows.

West Chester Performing Arts Center presented a full season of music and theater, and its schedule was, by all accounts in the major papers, at the level of most urban venues. Its members sought for it the feel of a Tanglewood or a Saratoga. Last season they'd scored an RSC traveling production of *Twelfth Night* and a Special Evening with James Taylor. For the summer, the board of directors voted to sprout an impromptu side venue, a smaller and more intimate setting for a series of special events. It was a coup to land a performance by Nyoto Kanata, the prodigy pianist. A three-day break between her performances at the Philadelphia Museum of Art had afforded WCPAC the opportunity to slot in a culturally important afternoon recital; the only minor gamble was that it would have to be the first Sunday in May. Risky weather. Though it was not her idea, Emily, who was on the programming committee, had been in favor of going to the extra expense of erecting the tent;

she saw how a small program of more experimental works would give the center a boost. She had taken increasing ownership of the effort and even found a friend in the catering business, who found a wedding planner, who found a construction guy, who put up the tent and got 250 seats comfortably inside. The board found enough dollars in the budget to allow for orchids and a small rock path. The stage area had the simple feel of a Japanese garden.

"Nyoto's adorable," Emily said. She was holding Ann's hand, sitting to her left. Her father reappeared, taking the empty chair on the other side.

"It doesn't look good out there," said Collier.

"We'll be fine," said Emily.

Ann said, "I don't need any water." Collier and Emily shared quick, pleased looks. Her split seconds of lucidity often presented like this: situational responses and statements completely in rhythm with the commonplace. The moments were like wine at a church party, welcome and rare.

"Nyoto spent the night at the Hilton," said Emily. "We had a little dinner at Tom Benton's. She's really very lovely, and completely polite." She leaned closer to make sure no one could hear. "She didn't say a word."

"Probably doesn't speak English," Collier said, trawling for reading glasses in his sport coat. Emily hated that jacket, a brown plaid weave with a dreadful light-blue stitch throughout. It was what he wore for years to anything he did not really want to go to; it was his way of signaling that a visit to Phil's parents' house or attending a school play was against his plans. He stuck his head in the program, making Emily feel like a gossip for commenting on Nyoto. She was only trying to keep her mother's mind focused by narrating things.

———

Emily my dear sweet girl she doesn't mean to be so hard on people my full love black-haired girl just like my father so much she pulls me down from the truck car touches my pearls and my sweater. No more rain mommy don't you look sweet let me take your pocketbook, there come down easy John says oop de doop and I'm out of car good John helping me hero john put his nice coat Emily walking through hallways carpet talking at me where's Johnny he's parking the car don't worry mom she is so worried heavy with worry she holds my arms and shows me where how to keep her from being a gloomy I always say to John I'll never know pass by the faces and pushing to seats Emily so anxious not stopping when we see the Butlers stop Big Ted says hi Annie how ya feelin' and Helen whispering to Emily on my side smile at Teddy always such a lovely fella looked like Fred MacMurray. It's a tent how about that a tent a big top everyone is tromping their wet inside the grass is patted into paths under the feet and plastic to walk through we've got seats right near the front mom Emily pushes my elbow. Her father is a complicated man that men are complicated we can't know that so poor thing she two-times can't know she can't know like a parent she doesn't think right about men like her father or the others. Here we go Mom John is back with us you know my John looks like Jimmy Stewart I'd tell him and he'd say bah honey you're full of soup I set down with them on my either side and they talk to people but not each other save a few words like I am not there what's the matter sweetheart he says but he knows I know when they talk like I'm not there and he knows that he tangles his arm through my arm and holds my hand.

———

"She speaks perfectly fine English, Dad," said Emily.

"Well, good," Collier said, dropping it. He was happy he had gotten Ann and himself there on time and in one piece. He had promised himself he would be sweet to Emily today, but she was putting him to the test.

Now she was whispering a rundown of the names of the people passing through the aisles. "Mr. and Mrs. Butler said hi," she said, trying to make up for snapping at him. He grunted. Emily knew damn well Ann could not follow what she was saying and would not have a clue who the people were anyway. He looked up toward the front of the tent and surveyed the concert apparatus before him to try to get a sense of exactly what his daughter had conjured up. The folding chairs were arranged amphitheatrically, and the piano, shiny as patent-leather Sunday shoes, stood on a square section of hardwood that had been put down to serve as a stage. He squinted to see if it was just a caterer's rental. He supposed a really professional outfit would have its own floor. The light in the room — if the inside of a tent could be called a room — was gauzy and yellow. The painted pine of the folding chairs, the grass ruined beneath all the loafers and pumps, and the sound of the plastic tarp doors zipping closed created the mood of a wedding crossed with a town-hall meeting. It had the same air as all local events striving to be fancy, and that, he thought to himself as Emily bent her mother's ear, was just the problem with everything the WCPAC put on.

Taking care of Ann since the stroke should not have been such a tug-of-war, such a contest of wills. It began before they had even left the hospital, with Emily speaking to the doctors alone, the nurses smiling at Collier and making small talk, only discussing how Ann slept and the changes in medication when his daughter arrived. He wondered how it had come to be that his child distrusted him so when it came to her mother. Before the thought got away, it was replaced with the reply that Emily had never forgiven him for years of inattentiveness. The day that Ann fell and the ambulance had to rush her in to Saint Joseph's, Emily took to the hospital room, sized up her mother, and shot her father a look that told him he could no longer pretend he had not ignored everything that ever mattered. He had no one to tell the way he felt since that moment: that his own little girl could reach that point was a helluva thing.

Regardless of the hurt, he worried again about rain for Emily's sake. Collier knew she'd be disappointed about the music, but he could also tell she had made the event personal, its success essential to her self-esteem in this moment. Emily rode the fence between risk and hope, which she got, respectively, from him and from her mother. In pushing all the special programs—here, take this Japanese kid playing classical piano in a tent in early May—his daughter was surely being hopeful, having faith that the needle could be threaded. But, unlike her mother, Emily was simultaneously burdened with Collier's gloomy foreboding. He saw that she had picked up his ability to disguise a punishing sense of doom with patronizing precautions, and he listened silently to her explaining to her uncomprehending

107

mother how she had hedged the upside of pulling something special off with contingency plans full of shuttle buses and breakdown crews.

Emily had offered to pick Ann up, hinting, not in a nice way, that Collier would prefer skipping the concert, as though the pressure of the show combined with the weight of having him along, bored and crotchety, was too much for her. He couldn't be too angry. Truth be told, he had a long record of avoiding this type of thing. While he had always had a feel for music—with a bit of gin, he could move away from any day with Sinatra—he just couldn't appreciate classical music. It had nothing to do with being unbending. He had done that bit, obligingly playing the part for two generations of the square old guy who didn't have the capacity for Bruce Springsteen or Eminem. His lack of feeling for refined music, like symphonies and string quartets and so forth—this was different. It was a door he could never open. Collier remembered trying over the years, remembered wanting to get what all the interest in Van Cliburn was over or what it was that made people cry at operas. He had never found a way to be inside the pounding chords of Beethoven, had felt doubly insensitive agonizing at the flinty twinkling high notes of Chopin that Emily had played at her recitals. He'd gone with Ann to the symphony in Philadelphia—gone to the trouble of putting in for the corporate tickets— and watched the devoting heads and tuxedoed torsos of a visiting European orchestra. Like a Picasso—or mesclun salad—he just didn't get it and felt like it was wasted on him. He wondered if it was genetic in nature or if it had to do with his engineer's training or if maybe he had just had some level of sensitivity beaten out of him in the army and over thirty years at GE.

One of the burning fires he had with Emily was how narrow-minded she thought he was. He didn't bother to tell her that when he went to school, even if it was for engineering in the fifties, they studied the classics a lot more than her crowd of competitive art-community types did. The generation in the middle—that era of people Emily's age—was so self-righteous about their schooling, as though the bright-line wrongs, the Jim Crow laws, and the pigeonholing of women in the house disqualified the entire edifice of their parents' education. Yet Collier was sure he'd learned more in college about concertos and intermezzos and Wagner and Liszt—or at least it had certainly been stressed more—than she had picked up in the spaces between gender studies, Native American history, and all the boyfriends.

———

Interviewer:
You've been performing since you were a very small girl. Do you still get nervous?
Interpreter:
(There is a pause while the interpreter listens to Nyoto speak in Japanese.) She says that when she was a young child, she was very frightened. Also she says that the first time she was away from her parents—it was on a trip to Europe when she was nine years old—she was very anxious each time she went to the stage. It was especially scary in Vienna, she says. Because the music is of so many composers of that place.

Interviewer:

Is she...Nyoto, are you enjoying your time in the United States?

Interpreter:

(Pause.) Yes, very much. (Pause.) She says she feels very happy to be able to bring her music to this place.

Interviewer:

How do you feel when you go on stage before a big crowd? And is it different for her when the audiences vary in musical knowledge?

Interpreter:

(Pause.) Could you repeat the question?

Interviewer:

Yes. I'm sorry. I guess what I'm asking is if she knows the difference between a crowd at the Philharmonic, for example, and an audience that may not be familiar with the music she plays?

Interpreter:

(There is a long delay while Nyoto speaks this time.)

She says there is a sound that a crowd makes when it shifts to quiet. It is like the hum of minds overtaking the noise of bodies. It is into this sound that musicians play. It may seem in this way that the music is like water filling an empty cup. Only this picture is wrong—the emptiness of the cup is an illusion. A cup is never empty. It is full of the air; other times it may be full of water, but it is not full of nothingness. Even the air is something. The air may be pushed out by *the water—and it will appear like something is replacing nothing. But it is not that way. The cup, which seemed empty, in truth had air all around, inside and out. When I begin to play for an audience, I think I am adding to the air. Nothing more. (Pause, while Nyoto says one last thing.) And, of course, I am hoping it will be beautiful.*

Interviewer:

Well, it is quite a treat for us to have you here. Thank you very much.

———

The lights, which had been intended for the recital's conclusion at twilight but were turned on early because of the darkness of the storm, came down. Emily shook her head in mock disbelief. "Everyone has worked so hard," she whispered to Ann. "I'm just so proud of them." It felt great to say the sweet things, to fill up the spaces between moments with happy, positive small talk, as her mother had always been the first to do. And she knew they were being watched by all of them, all the busybodies who had nothing better to do but gauge how bad Ann was since they'd seen her last. Emily looked at her father, who stared at the stage, abdicating the role of custodian now that he was not the only one to whom Ann was entrusted. It was just like him to beg off and go into a cocoon as soon as Emily arrived. He couldn't dump Ann quickly enough and get back to his subterranean preoccupations, whatever they were.

Emily had long since stopped feeling sorry for Collier, but she did get wistful for them both. When she was a girl, he was so distinct and memorable, telling her elephants were blue and going into great detail about a special planet just for alligators. She remembered the mornings when Ann's job at the hospital required her to leave before breakfast so her dad would sneak out and bring home a half dozen Dunkin' Donuts and they would try to eat three each. He came to Emily's room every night at bedtime and read a story, often shutting the book to talk about the events of the day and then waiting for her to fall asleep. But that man had not been around for a very long time.

It was not that he had changed suddenly; he had never been carefree or light. That was Ann. But he had worsened; after he retired it was as though his excitement to *do* things—to go to the park, to drive to the shore, or to go to the movies—had drained away. Where her mother would take a watercolor class or announce that she was going to make tacos, her father shrank into a smaller and smaller set of patterns, not telling stories or gossiping about corporate shuttling at GE and giving up golf. He was like a painting that became less interesting and more faded as it aged. Her father was the one person she could think of who became more of a type and less of a distinct character as time wore on, disappearing into a cheap brown sport coat and withdrawing into an ever less interesting and reductive world.

It was against this backdrop of Collier's fading distinctness, four years before Ann's stroke, that Emily decided to leave her husband, Phil. "Men are just built that way," Ann had said in a last-ditch effort to talk Emily out of it. The way her mother's lower lip had quivered— just for a fraction of an instant—was enough for Emily to know there had been some tough water somewhere in her parents' marriage that had not leaked out to her. The divorce with Phil was brutal, especially with three little kids involved, but Emily was determined not to leave her life to hope.

Once it was clear her daughter would not change her mind about the breakup, Ann, in classic Ann fashion, simply showed up for her grandkids more often, making it a custom to stop by every day with such a supply of calm, direct, predictable affection that Emily was able to take the time — moments, days, weekends — needed to mourn her marriage and heal. Yet no matter how amazing Ann proved to be, Emily knew she didn't want her mother's life: putting up with a distant man falling further down a hole as the years went by.

There was a murmur at the left of the stage, and the tiniest little thing in a black fitted dress entered Emily's depth of field. Nyoto Kanata walked to the piano and sat down at the bench. Catching herself, like an actor who had forgotten a line, Nyoto stood back up and took a step toward the crowd. She bent her head and gave a quick wave, head and hand going in opposite directions. Then she smiled, and several pops of light went off. Emily growled to herself, angry that a few bad apples had ignored the rule against flash photography.

"*Rolla alla turtunda,*" said Nyoto, and she turned back to the piano.

Just as Emily feared, her father leaned across her mother and said, too loudly, "What'd she say?"

Would ya feel the queer browning light under this bigtop sky there is still sunlight from the openings and peeking in under the sides where the straps haven't held the canvas down hope we don't blow away I say I tell them I don't need water. There she is Emily points and a teeny tiny little girl, a little oriental girl walks up to the piano they have sitting in the front of the folding chairs and the people start clapping and the claps thud into the sides of the folding walls and it goes hush just as fast John squeezes my hand and sits up straight like he does when he pays attention and his mind clears from all side cloudy points and gets about thinking of that only one thing.

———

When Nyoto touched the piano for the first time, nothing happened. Collier looked at Emily, who tensed up like a bird dog. Both relaxed as a sound came though the tent. It was a simple musical phrase, to be sure, but unlike anything Collier had heard before. It was a curved noise without edges; it was not the sharp and disinviting tincture he associated with the angry piano of classical concerts. His range of vision narrowed to the one focal point the stage allowed: a pink rose next to the root of Nyoto's column of hair. It formed the top of a right triangle, with her waist and the keyboard sitting at the other points. For an instant, Nyoto withdrew her hands as though they'd almost been snatched by a closing jewelry box, and this time Collier's worry was not just that the WCPAC crew had small-timed it but also that something profound was in motion that he did not want to stop. Nyoto's pullback was just a flourish, and for a second time her fingers made contact with the keys to issue a soothing and dulcet combination of notes. Everything—every thought and every light—began to vanish, like the moment of anesthesia when anxieties begin to melt away.

Collier's engineer's mind pushed back. What the little girl was playing couldn't have been a high-quality piece: it was too accessible to him. Maybe this was a B version of classical music. Emily had said it was going to be Mozart, and he suddenly wondered if Mozart had become too popularized and—with things like the *Baby Mozart* books and DVDs—the music had become commoditized such that the great heights of intelligence one had to possess to appreciate it had been reduced. Quickly, though, his mind's eye closed down and the rest of him gave over to the emotion of the sound, the way random thoughts about the level of the light or the need for mood or more wine recede as lovemaking begins. He looked at Ann, who stared straight ahead. Nyoto's shoulders swayed as her hands glided over the keys. Ann squeezed Collier's hand much the way she might have twenty years before. He bit his lip lightly— his way of fending off emotion. Ann could not hear the music—he knew that. She was going on things unheard: instinct, the feeling of the crowd, and the spirit of the faces. Her smile widened as she looked back at him now and picked up on his gaze. She was the most kind, the most happy, the most steadily happy girl in the world.

The first canvasy tap from above hit unmistakably, and his heart dipped. He tried to ignore it, the way a six-year-old left fielder ignores the first raindrop at a Saturday ball game. The afternoon's storm was back. He knew it would now hit them hard, and he knew it with the same surety that he knew his beautiful, thinning, deteriorating, and nearly deaf wife was dying. The big top popped with noise now, and the crowd could be felt resisting the urge to look up. Its kindly effort—not that of the big city—to suspend disbelief and forestall the storm gave way as the rattle became louder and louder yet, until it was all the assembly could hear. Wind from outside blew the plastic tarp doors against their zippers and away from their ties. Collier saw Emily put her hands on her knees and look to the left and right, searching for other committee members with whom she could make eye contact, telegraphing the question of whether something had to be done and whether someone had to call off the fun.

Nyoto continued playing undaunted. Collier felt her interweaving the different storylines of the piece, momentum building. Her head rose and her eyes closed with the movement of the arrangement; just as quickly she brought her forehead back down, and her gaze returned to the keys. To his amazement, the chaotic and insistent noise of the rain was countermanded by a new surge of harmony. Ann, the gathering's other undisturbed soul, was beaming now, still staring straight ahead. The rain and the notes fused together in a blend of color and vibration and light.

Emily began to make her way toward the aisle in the other direction, leaving them alone. Soon others, bent politely at the waist, started heading to the exits, thinking about shuttle buses and traffic and getting out of the lot, of postponements and theater series make-goods, of what a bad idea it was to throw this tent up in the first place, especially this early in the year. And, still, Ann looked forward, connected to Nyoto, who played on. Collier focused on his wife's eyes. The rain was unstoppable, not slowing enough even to divide into drops. Nyoto swayed more heavily. Collier believed for the first time since Ann had left him that he was with her: in her thoughts, her feelings, her interpretation of this world and the next. It was all wrapped together. He heard nothing and everything all at once. Whatever he had failed to understand before — stupidly and selfishly — he understood now.

Starting Out

On a Monday morning in November 1988, Oscar Rothbart pointed at a yellow Post-it note stuck to my faux-leather, semi reclining, office-grade chair on the twenty-first floor of the Citibank Tower in downtown Los Angeles. I was unfocused. It was 10:13 a.m., and I was just getting into my office. Or I was getting into "our office," since this particular eight-by-ten-foot "junior executive exterior" was also occupied by Rothbart, a French Canadian who started at the firm with me on the same day.

For the first time anyone could remember, through some mistake in planning, some HR fuckup, the twenty-odd new lawyers were paired together in offices. It was April, and we had been sharing since we'd started in the fall. Beginning work at a major law firm seemed strikingly similar to other education cycles: the randomly assigned roommate, the orientation meetings, the new class of people, and the older guys who talked about how great everything used to be. It was like school in these ways but different. This was the mystical real world we'd all been warned about, and, bit-by-bit, it sunk in that the fun of college and the dress rehearsal of law school were done. Some embraced it, and some recoiled. The ones who had been forty years old their whole lives settled in; the eight-year-olds panicked. Playtime was over.

Rothbart looked up. "Hank came here *himself* looking for you." He had been named after Oscar Wilde by anthropologist parents in Montreal. "And your phone rang twice."

Our crowded office struck a contrast to the venerable solitude of the firm. Green carpets and dark walnut trim defined the corridors and lobbies, along with brass lamps, framed clipper ships, and old-time *Vanity Fair* portraits of solicitors. Rothbart's side was minimalist, as he was extremely anticlutter. He had a glass desk, and it smelled of antiseptic, which smelled to me like work. The only thing on it was draft interrogatory responses he'd been marking up since he arrived, as he did on all days, at seven. By the time I stumbled in, he'd done as much as I would do in a week. He was a machine, cranking out the mindless work product of a first-year associate. Rumor had it he was already doing footnotes on one of Dave Van Wyck's appellate briefs. He was, by all accounts, going places.

He was postmodern and sarcastic, and he liked right angles. He was one of those people always chewing gum but not a full piece—just a tiny speck of gray momentarily visible between his molars. He looked the part: average height, good looks, striking designer eyewear. His body was in great shape, as befits the disciplined barrister on the ladder of success. He was natty, treading the line between downtown boring and Westside stylish. He knew to get one-inch cuffs on his pants. His shirts were crisp, he had good ties, and, following a maxim he'd read in *Vogue* ("If you want to know if a man is well dressed…look down"), he had great shoes.

"Thanks," I said.

"Busy night?"

"Nothing special," I said, which was true. This was my first nonhourly job, and I was drunk with the power of being on my own time. I had stayed out till the bars were almost closed and then ran to the convenience store in time to get a six-pack and cigarettes, which I finished off on the patio of my place in west LA. I liked to drink and read late. It was 9:08 when I woke, and, like all days, I rushed to take a shower and made it downtown by quarter after ten, which I thought was the latest I could arrive without making someone in a position of power notice.

"What do you think Hank wants?" asked Rothbart.

"I don't know, Oscar. He wants to see me, as you know from reading my note. You tell me what he wants."

"I think he's going to fire your ass."

This was typical shit for Oscar. It is amazing how well you get to know a roommate, even in a few months and even if he's just an officemate in the Torts, Insurance, and Business Litigation Group at the LA office of a 2,100-lawyer global powerhouse. But I had the same thought. The yellow Post-it note was a death warrant. Rothbart knew instinctively I was scared well beyond the usual yips of a low-grade beer-vodka, rocks-cigarette hangover. He spun in his semi reclining, office-grade chair and took aim between my eyes.

"You know, Yates, you really need to bring some maturity to bear. We make one hundred seventy-five thousand dollars a year, and they're not going to put up with it much longer." He paused and then smirked.

"And frankly, I don't think they should. Hank and Rusty are pulling a discovery team together for TCE, and it's going to change from there. It's being fast-tracked, and I'm hearing we are going with a way, way scaled-back approach. It's smart: this way Anderson and the other plaintiffs' lawyers can't jam Hank and TCE's general counsel on fees. Rusty told me we'll be doing three simultaneous depo tiers in Sacramento, and they have a deal on corporate housing—three apartments in a nice complex. Should be all summer. Totally sweet billables."

"Did you just say 'totally sweet billables'?" I said.

"Laugh all you want, chief." He said "chief" like a regular Canadian, but it was affected. Then, not being able to help himself, he continued, "By the way, in case you didn't know, I have this complete piece of ass from Newport who's up there doing an internship, so I will be getting fucked, too." He was proud of himself for this; he talked about his prowess with girls a little too much. "What about you? You're out in the cold. Doesn't that scare you?"

"I have the Lifetime Fund case with Amy and Andy," I said, referring to two young partners who had me on a case so big they couldn't keep tabs on what I was doing.

"Ha," he snorted. "Take it from me: Amy and Andy are getting canned any day."

"How the fuck do you know that?"

"Because I get information, fuck face. Because I get here at seven and do whatever anyone tells me to do. Because I don't get drunk every night and read novels till three in the morning." He squinted and lifted his palms. "Do you ever get, like, past anything? You're so *stuck*."

Perhaps the only thing that made our relationship

interesting is that we were both English majors in college and would kill time talking about books and movies and art and music. He went to Yale and Yale Law School, facts that solidified my disposition toward him. He did his college thesis on Phillip Glass and abstract art and his law-review comment on critical legal studies. I really didn't like anything about him, but I ended up spending so much time in his presence I felt like I was stuck to him. He annoyed me and made me feel insufficient, but I sat there and took it. He told me once I was banal, putting the accent on the second syllable. I'd never heard it pronounced that way before. When I fought back, defending the inherent truth of a movie or novel or record, he'd mock me for so much "pathos." I usually just gave in to his confidence.

After I pretended to work for a while, I tried to change the subject. "I watched *The Last Waltz* the other day. What do you think of Rick Danko? You know, from The Band."

"The one who was always so drunk?"

"They were all kind of drunk."

"True." I watched him mull it over. "I know who you're talking about. He sang 'It Makes No Difference.'" Rothbart zeroed in. "He was a drug addict. Killed himself, right?"

"No, that was one of the other guys."

"Well, he's a minor figure, and they were overrated." Now he made air quotes and said, in a mocking voice, "'The Band. Ooooh. They're so great.' Give me a break." He paused. "Dylan was probably at his worst with those guys."

"Perfect."

"Why? What do you think of him? You're going to tell me there's any *other* thing to think?"

"Well, yeah…I watch that movie and think, like… he was too sweet to live in this world."

He looked at me for a second and then jumped out of his chair. "That's it!"

"That's *what*?"

"That's your problem. You actually *think* that." He sat down and settled in for a speech with all the melodrama that office politics can offer. "Let me tell you something. We've been in this office awhile, but I don't *really* give a rat's ass about you. I'm not your friend, I'm not your buddy, and, candidly, I think you have behavioral issues. But since I don't think I will be stuck with you much longer, I will give you one piece of sorely needed advice. Are you ready?"

"Yeah."

"Sentimentality is dead. It's for losers. Everything—art, politics, whatever—has moved past it. Look around you. You're in *business*. You should have learned this by now."

———

Some girls remind you of songs, and some girls remind you of bands. Joyce had straight blue and black hair with creamy brown eyes and a raspy voice from smoking cigarettes, all of which killed me dead. I'd had a crush on Joyce for nine years by now. We lived in the same dorm at Cornell and then ended up in the same class at law school at NYU. She had been on the law review and got a job with a federal judge in LA, which caused her, too, to be stuck downtown. We were East Coasters who had been through a lot together, from Western civ to con law and from keg parties and bongathons to doing bumps of coke in the bathrooms of Greenwich Village bars.

I met her a little past noon in the elevator lobby, and we descended into the bowels of the Citibank center to the food court, a circle of fast-food emporiums with names like Hunan Pride, Soup N Salad, Thai Dishes, and Uno Pizzeria. We rode the elevator with two highly accessorized black girls who threw their shoulders back as they walked. I said hi, and they smiled.

"Black girls in offices are always shitty until you talk to them," I told Joyce as we walked. "Then they're nice."

"Shut up," she said. "Someone might hear you."

We sat on white plastic chairs at a white plastic table made yellow in a few spots by cigarettes. We were surrounded by receptionists, people from IT departments, accounts-payable reps, and secretaries. The other guys at the firm went to work out at lunch, trying to stay in shape until, through the magic of corporate time, they had to work through lunch or take business lunches. "That's why older lawyers get fatter," one of the secretaries once told me. I usually just went to the food court, not understanding the appeal of a quick sweat and a shower.

Joyce liked me—Jewish girls always do—but she didn't need me. When we were sophomores, I had her shirt off in the backseat of a car on the way home from a concert in Buffalo, but she was drunk. Her friends took her home, and then she didn't look at me for a month. Our friendship soldiered on and was deep and complicated, and somewhere along the line we reached old-buddy status. Only I missed out on the sex. She was smarter than me, and I could never get her. We fought like crazy over the years, and I think that is what prevented me from really getting into her pants. More

125

than anything, she had to be right, and if she never fucked me, she would always win.

But as we matured, we gained respect for each other. Unlike me, Joyce had a great work ethic. I breezed by in classes without much work. She took great notes; I never took notes. I would come to her for study lists, and she would come to me for the right twist of phrase for a paper or a brief. We often talked about what we wanted to do. And now we were here in the inferno of the food court in the West, far away from our homes.

She had lousy taste in men. She had even dated Rothbart. Her first boyfriend in California was named Jay, and he was in television. He was five feet five, talked fast, and called me "brotha." She'd moved on to a new guy who worked at Paramount. I met him once, Brandon something, a few years older and from Beverly Hills. Like most of the Hollywood people I met, Brandon determined within thirty seconds of meeting someone whether anything was at stake, and if not, he moved on. I had no way of understanding these people, these rude and ruthless motherfuckers. They seemed like they must be kidding. I thought the whole town needed a good beating. I told Joyce we had not set out from Ithaca for her to end up with snivelers like this.

But I was at least happy she was no longer dating Rothbart, whom she had met with me at one of the many office functions thrown by the firm. To my amazement, they had a nice conversation, which led to an exchange of numbers and then several months of dating. I hadn't really let her off the hook for it.

"What was it like?" I asked.

"What was *what* like?"

"You know…going out with him. *Being* with him. You know."

"Oh Jesus, this again." She made a look like she was searching for the exit.

I pushed. "Did you ever get the feeling he was gay?"

"He's not gay." She thought about it a little more. "Who knows what he is? I thought he was cute. He *is* cute, Frankie. And, you know, he says Yale's not the best place for Jews. We talked about that. I thought he was, like, angry and vulnerable but couldn't show it. It was interesting to me. What can I say?"

I worked on not being bothered by it. Still, try as I might, I was obsessed: about his game, his rap, and what would make this beautiful, smart, and funny girl fall for it. I was ashamed of being so juvenile, but I had to know what convinced her to go for him.

"I've only told you ten million times it was a six-week mistake. The kind I always make." She waved her hand. "He is a freak. Every minute of every day is organized. I mean, you wake up on a Saturday, and he's out of bed by eight. One time, we went to a club…like some techno club—"

"You went to a techno club?"

"I'm ignoring you. We were out till three, and he was still up at eight. He plays with the dog in his yard till eight twenty—it's that organized. Look, in that moment I was *impressed*, even *hopeful*, seeing that he even *had* a dog. It's not easy to think of him thinking of anything else. But then I got that, too—the dog is like a…like an artifice, y'know? There by design, like everything else— like the photo of Derrida in his bathroom."

"He has a photo of Jacques Derrida in his bathroom?"

"A little one. I know. Good God, right? I mean, who even knows who he is? I wonder if Brandon knows who he is," she said, drifting for a second. "So, *anyway*, it's till eight twenty with the dog, and then he eats some super-healthy breakfast—berries and grain or something. He did make me coffee. I think he was turned off that I had coffee…that meant I wasn't a super-healthy eater. Then he goes to his Pilates class, then the dry cleaner, and then he's home. He takes a shower, and then he's off to a 'Saturday lunch.' He always has lunch on Saturday with someone—I think it's where he conducts his real long-term plans. Lots of Hollywood people. That's his big plan, whether he admits it or not, like everybody out here. He just won't admit it yet because it would make him like every other schmuck out here. Plus, those guys all do shit jobs at the beginning."

I couldn't take it anymore. "How could you stomach having sex with him?"

"Oh, stop." She gave me a bent-knuckled middle finger. "You fucking baby." She smiled. She was brilliant. She got so disappointed in me at times like this, and it was at times like this that I loved her best.

She became wistful. "You know, my father says we sometimes end up spending a lot of time throughout our lives with certain people—and we just look up one day and realize we don't have a good reason for it. They may have been people we were assigned to or knew in a past life, or maybe we just saw them at magic hour one day when they were beautiful."

"But what happens?"

"Maybe we're just too lazy to shake them off."

"Yeah, maybe," I said.

She was still wistful and looking away. "It's really hard for girls, you know." She was always looking away from me. "You just look back sometimes and think of a guy and say, 'Did I really blow him?'"

"I think you need to get out of LA."

"I do, too. The guys here are terrible."

"Since when do you define yourself by men?"

"Oh, please...nice try. Tell that to my mother."

"What about Brandon?"

"You guys are all on one of two roads. It's boring." She put on her sunglasses—the big kind—and we cleared our trays. "Come with me. I have to pick up fucking panty hose—can you believe it? The Judge makes us come to court in hose. Walk with me?" As she grabbed my arm, she lost her balance for a second and accidentally rubbed her breast on my arm. It was one of those awkward moments that electrifies a guy and can't be shrugged off. We locked eyes for a second. Then she said, "C'mon, tough guy. Walk with me." And she pulled me away.

———

As the time for my appointment drew near, I looked around my office. There were five boxes of Amy and Andy's case files filling up my half of the space. They made Rothbart nuts, because he had those Felix Unger instincts. They made me crazy for a different reason. I had represented for months that I had been reviewing them—that I had encyclopedic knowledge of their contents. A hedge fund somewhere had probably paid eighty thousand dollars for the phony hours I had billed to those boxes. Even making a master list was hard for me because I was so bored and scattered: bank documents, loan agreements, copies of deeds of trust, promissory notes, UCC-1 filings, and lengthy, contentious letters between banks and law firms about the underlying loan documents and deeds of trust and UCC-1s and promissory notes.

Every time I opened one of the boxes I was overcome with powerful confusion. I stared at the words and saw my death amid the death of the imagination they represented. When I read promissory notes, I felt my body flying backward, pulled toward the window, then out in the sky above Figueroa Street, and finally into one those black-and-white death spirals you saw in old movies. I talked to myself, saying things like "a real promissory note is *I will love you forever*" and "the goal of the law is to kill all ambiguity." The truth was that I was nothing but ambiguity and romanticism and hadn't figured out my life. I wasn't ready to kill all ambiguity. This was a world that allowed no creativity, no flirting with juror number three, and no songs — none. This was the business world, and it was for greedy cunts like Oscar.

Rothbart came flying back into the office, his hair wet from the lunch workout. "Cameron had an interview at Disney. Can you believe it? Lucky prick. I knew it. I knew he wasn't serious about this place."

"Is that a good job?"

"Are you serious? Business affairs at a studio like Disney? Everybody wants that — at least anybody who's awake. One hundred eighty-five grand to start, and with stock options. And you're in the game."

"Yeah, but you'll still be a lawyer. I thought you wanted to be a real downtown lawyer — a person connected to the world of letters, flying to New York and all that crap."

"You're an idiot." He went back to the interrogatories.

"Wow, Oscar." I had a creeping feeling that Rothbart had outsmarted me. "I don't believe you. I'm here listening to you all day—that is, the few hours I can stand to be here. And I guess, well, yeah, I did believe that at least you liked it here—I mean, enough to get here at seven and kiss ass the way you do."

"Duuuude." He laughed and stopped working. "Frankie. Big boy. I like it: you're so sincere." He grinned some more, as if he were discovering something. "I like it." He put his hands over his head and put his feet up. "I guess today is the day when it all comes out...you *must* be getting fired. That would explain all the drama."

But he stopped right before he was going to lay into me. He went in another direction. "You know, there's this crazy thing that sticks in my mind every time I see you or think about you. Do you know what it is? It is so juvenile; I've always loved it. It's absurdist. It's like John Cage meets Keith Haring meets *The Benny Hill Show*. It captures so much while being so stupid." He looked to see if any of this had registered. "I just have this memory of when Cornell came to New Haven for the football game my junior year. We had this guy who would walk around the Yale Bowl during that game with a sandwich sign—you know, front and back. The front says *The Big Red*, and then you see the back when he walks by, and it says *Gives Head*. Ha! How great is that?"

This is how bad it gets, I said to myself. "Look, dude, don't go down this road." I was trying not to take the bait. "And you're avoiding my question. You want to work at a studio? That's it for you? That's the play for you? You have acted for the past ten months as though this job is your whole future. Are you serious about anything? Do you ever tell the truth? Do you know the truth?"

He raised his eyebrows in mock discovery. "My God, it is true: *The Big Red Gives Head.*" He was laughing. "Rick Danko. Christ, even the song is called 'It Makes No Difference.'" He was laughing hard now. I was still hung over. "You're about to get fired, so I shouldn't even waste my time with you. But since we're such good friends, I will give you some even better advice."

"More advice? Aside from the 'no sentimentality' speech from this morning, you douchebag?"

"Right, Lord Byron. After no sentimentality, no self-pity, no drunkenness, no art, no Rick Danko, no 'Papa's banquet wasn't big enough'—after all those things that define you, all the reasons why you're getting fired—after all of that, there's another rule. Maybe this one will help you in your next life."

I knew on some level he was right about something. I had no defense but sarcasm. "Oh yeah, well, what's that, Oscar? Help me."

"Don't be so sincere, Yates." He was quiet, like he was really trying to help me. "It's always a mistake. Don't ever say what you mean. It opens you up to attacks. There's always a deeper truth to protect, chief. You think I'm staying here with these Pasadena fucks?"

———

Hank Dowling's secretary told me to come by at half past three. Her name was Connie, and she was a chesty California blonde pushing sixty. I saw a picture of her on the White House lawn in 1970, and she was smoking hot. She had gone to work in the Nixon administration in 1968, when guys from SC ran the world and banged secretaries who looked like Connie. She was a nice lady, and I had always gone out of my way to talk to her—to be decent, really. A secretary in a world given over to legal assistants, she ran Hank's life, and he ran everyone else's.

I was petrified by the thought of being fired. I was ok at the job when I focused; I just couldn't focus. I calmed myself by thinking of my assets. There were a lot of jocks at the firm, and I was a good ballplayer, so I had it pretty easy, as ridiculous as that was. I threw a guy out at third from right field in a big softball game when I was a summer clerk, and that made me golden. Afterward we would drink with Hank and Rusty and Dave Van Wyck at the John Bull Pub in Pasadena, and from then on I was part of that tradition. I now realize that, more often than not, if you scratch a partner in a big law firm or CEO or vice chairman, underneath you will find a ballplayer, especially in Southern California and especially outside Hollywood. Good ballplayers go a long way.

I started to prepare myself for my new life should I get fired. I could try to get another job or even try something I was interested in, like teaching or writing. Just then, Connie called me. My life has been full of women like Connie, patron saints along the road— repayment for waving the incense as an altar boy, I liked to think. She told me to be there at half past three, but at 3:34 when I arrived, Hank was on the phone, so she said to have a seat on a chair outside his door. He had a coffee-table book on Salvador Dalí, and I turned to *Figure at a Window*. It's a painting of his sister at a window before an endless sea. Dalí did it before he went bat-shit crazy with eyeballs and melting watches.

As I sat waiting, Connie looked at me and said, "You're all right." Then she went back to her typing. It was just a moment. I started wondering whether it was real or not—whether I had imagined it.

Connie's phone buzzed, and she said, "Go in. He's off the phone."

Banks with bad loans, automakers with fuel-fire victims, and billionaires with mouthy mistresses—they all came to Hank Dowling. He was a huge guy from Nebraska who'd been a marine for two tours in Vietnam before going to law school and becoming a hometown prosecutor. He got restless and chased pussy to LA, where he settled into the business bog and became a successful defender of corporate malfeasance. He played rugby and went fly-fishing and had bona fide real-man credentials at a time when young men were being called metrosexuals. At cocktail parties he said "fuck" and drank brown liquor, and he made us feel like being a lawyer for international corporations was the best goddamn thing you could do. He was kind to custodians and secretaries and the shoeshine guy in the lobby.

"Come in, Frank. Sorry, that call took a little longer than I would have preferred."

"Oh hey, Hank, no problem. You looking for me?"

"Yeah. Gotta talk for a sec." He pointed at the door since he was already sitting back at his desk. "Shut that."

Not the best sign, I thought to myself. I sat on his sectional couch and looked at the ceramic award on the end table, too nervous to ascertain what it was. Given my mental state, I was satisfied with identifying the object on some rudimentary, cerebral-cortex level as a curved shape. Hank's couch sunk in so that when you sat on it you were about three feet below him.

"Frankie, I have a memo here from admin that says you don't have your time sheets in for the end of March. Now, I hate this shit, and I hate doing time sheets, too…but goddamn it, they give it to me to handle. You get my drift?"

"Oh gosh, Hank—shoot. I'm sorry. That's a big fuckup. I had them into the girl in word processing, and…" Then I stopped. I realized this was all it was. "You know what? Forget that. No excuses; this is on me. I will fix it, and it won't happen again."

He smoothed out. "Ok. Say no more." He leaned back. "There *are* too many goddamn rules around here; don't get me wrong." Smoother still, he said, "It's what happens with Democrats—I tell them that, the cocksuckers." Now he was laughing. "And by Democrats I mean New York. And by New York… well, you know what I mean by New York. They know how to make money." He shot me a wink. "Ah shit, I have fun with those guys—they're a little scared of me." He laughed at himself and got up to walk me out. "But listen, pal, let me give you some advice."

He had me by the arm at the door of his office. Then he put his mouth up to my ear and said quietly, "When you are a lawyer for a big firm, there is only one thing you must do. But you must do this one thing above all others."

"Yes, sir?"

"Do your fucking time sheets. It's how we make money. Don't shoot yourself in the foot. You're too good a guy to let these pricks get at you like that."

"I got it. I got it."

"Good." He guided me out the door. "Hey, I can't play tonight, but I will stop by the Bull for a few. I want you to catch me up on Amy and Andy's case — may need you to step up on that while some things change at the partner level."

"Of course."

"I just settled that TCE piece of shit, and we're going to have to phase out some of the young lawyers to other firms. Don't worry; they can probably go with Van Wyck and Rusty because they're setting up a new shop." He gave me a wink. "You're doing good." He grabbed my shoulder. "Now keep this all between me and you, copy?"

"Sure thing. See you tonight."

———

As the elevator transported me to my floor, I saw the alternatives, clear and unconfused. You may share an office, a bed, or a dorm room, but you don't share a coffin. I had done my time sheets for March, and I knew where Pasadena was. My hangover was gone, and I was ready for a beer. Amy and Andy were out, Joyce's clerkship would end, and no longer would I wonder if Connie had really spoken to me. I was safe, and if I wanted to, I could be safe for the next forty years. More than one door was open, and I could be as sincere or as sentimental as I wanted to be. Life would be good here in LA, far away from the East, New York, and Rothbart.

I walked back into our office. Rothbart looked up, dying for the news.

I stared at him. "You know, Oscar, I always wanted to ask you something."

"Yeah? What?"

"What was it *like* for you at Yale, you pussy?"

Miracle Worker

I.

Eliot Stevens started each day with the obituaries. As his sixties took hold, he came to understand that his preferred sections of the *New York Times* changed with the stages of his life: he had jumped straight to the sports pages as a boy, grew into the headlines at Colgate, fought with the op-eds during law school at Columbia, and settled into the adult life of a New Yorker with the "Business Day" section every Monday through Thursday and "Weekend" on Fridays. Saturdays the paper was of very little import—it was leaner, and there were errands to run. Sundays were an altogether different business, a block of work that could not be knocked out in one sitting. Now, though, he was firmly in a new part of life. He went right for the daily bios of the freshly dead, which could be found behind the stocks, near the crossword—on Tuesdays with the chess. The obituaries were his quotidian launchpad, a strange kind of comfort food he took in from the breakfast table in his townhouse on Eighty-Fourth Street just off of West End.

The stories were a part of life hidden in plain sight. It was as though Stevens, after years of walking past

Mexican restaurants, found tacos a revelation. He had never paid proper attention to the spice and flavors of the obituaries. He became a connoisseur of their specialty composition with all its moving parts. He savored the blunt headlines: "Dick Clark, American Entertainment Entrepreneur, dead at 82" and "Sumner LaPlante, Invented Corrugated Insulation." He evaluated the choice of photograph—whether the still of a soldier posed in silhouette in uniform or the publicity shot of a long-forgotten TV actor with a fedora and a .38 from a lesser police procedural of the 1960s.

Stevens analyzed the tactics the writers used to make each article seem original regardless of formula. He took a special pleasure in the longer pieces by master craftsmen like Albin Krebs, who would tease out the lead highlights and a quote or two and then smoothly double back to the obituaries' beginnings. This device was especially fun when the subject was an immigrant who had adopted an Americanized name. Krebs would announce the sad passing of, for instance, ventriloquist Willie Friedman, who was famous throughout the Poconos in the fifties and sixties, and then detail the showman's impressive longevity, making special mention of the delight audiences took in the dummies. With readers hooked and settled in with coffee and bran muffins, Krebs would take a storyteller's pause before continuing like so: "Walter Meryce Ferndhayl was born in Stuttgart, Germany, in 1921..."

Stevens knew, of course, that his increased attention to obituaries meant that part of him was dealing with big issues. But he was confident he was maintaining an objective sense—it wasn't all introspection and mortality. The paper seemed to be telling him to think about the brevity and arbitrariness of life and about change and loss. In an era when most news was consumed online, the quirkily styled signature pieces spread before him in newsprint represented a time when tastes were our own. The people who were dying off — the inventors of saran wrap and the Barbie doll and the apparently endless number of marines who had shot dozens of Japanese on Guadalcanal — were hardening day by day into symbols of what America used to be. In death they became objects, their earnest lives now complete, leaving the world that much less substantial.

He saw the obituaries as a victory lap for the subjects — their last bit of ticker tape — and as fundamentally *good* things, especially when regarded alongside their journalistic shadow, the death notices. Like the side of the graveyard reserved for prostitutes and gangsters, the death notices were relegated to the lower half of the facing page and had a want-ad type size and font. The citizens of the death-notice ghetto — even the nonagenarians whose families could afford the eulogies of five hundred words with their recitations of every prep school and homeowners' board and not-so-veiled anger that the subject had been denied a proper journalistic send-off — had been adjudicated to have not accomplished enough, at least as far as the coldhearted *Times*' obit editor was concerned, to make the grade. No matter whom you were, you could not manufacture a life in reverse that deserved to be obituarized. Something *special*, almost miraculous, had to have happened in your life.

There was no definition and no clear guidelines. The specialness could have come in an instant, like it did for Bobby Thompson, when he hit a home run against the

Dodgers in 1954, or it might have developed over seven decades, like Daniel Bell's intellectual engagement. Whether one rated an obituary was an easy call for Stevens once he became an *aficionado*. The qualification process reminded him of Justice Potter Stewart's famous take on pornography: "I know it when I see it." The chosen were of a class.

The only corruption Stevens could find concerned the city's oldest families. Every so often, a Whitney or Astor or Blaine descendant of no particular note would sneak in. Staying vigilant for this subspecies was like bird watching for Stevens. High-end sightings were delicious — they combined sober respect for the family's part in building Gotham with grisly details of falsified estate plans forced upon fading dowagers. Stevens would catch these gems and say to Maribeth, "Have to hand it to them," in reference to the dolts who had never worked a day in their lives. "They have something." Invariably, he received no response — Maribeth tried not to buy into what she considered a grim and melancholy hobby.

Like anybody, Stevens sometimes thought about whether the *Times* would print an obituary about him. He doubted he would make it much further than the *Carlton Tribune*, the local paper of the northern Pennsylvania town where he had grown up. He imagined the piece would mention that his father was a once-prominent doctor without, hopefully, intimating that the family hit upon hard times when the fortunes of the town declined. Any piece on Stevens would certainly mention his scholarship to Colgate, where he was a member of the eight-man sculls for three campaigns and graduated with honors in rhetoric, and that he became a lawyer, joining Mason Tate & Gathers in 1979. The ideal obituary would skip over the fact that he was rejected for partnership and instead would laud him for starting his own solo practice and maintaining it out of the same office on the twenty-sixth floor of the Empire State Building from 1985 until he died. Perhaps he would draw a compliment — maybe even a friendly quote from another attorney — about his tireless work as one of the legion of hardworking lawyers who had disentangled the mess around ground zero after 9/11.

As predictable as the form of a sales agreement, any story of Stevens' life would recite that he would be survived by his lovely wife, Maribeth; their son, Alex, a doctor (the medicine-man gene, like baldness, had skipped a generation); Alex's wife, Jennifer, also a doctor; and their little boy, Nicholas. And that was about it. He had done nothing notable to justify inclusion in the record as a standout. Stevens told himself that was just as well — that it didn't mean much to have been the author of cola jingles or a member of Meyer Lansky's crew. He imagined Maribeth would take out a small remembrance for him in the notices, maybe even mentioning his fondness for an orderly desk, collar pins, and — this would be her sense of humor — reading aloud the names and ages of the newly deceased from the paper in the morning.

As he looked out at the rain over Riverside Park on a gray day at his breakfast table, a death notice, lengthy even by the indulgent standards of the wealthy, jumped out at him:

BROWNING — Sr. Robert Joseph, 92, Wall Street legend, retired partner

of Allderdyce & Allen & Co., World
War II veteran, leading philanthropist,
humanitarian, mentor, cancer survivor,
heart attack survivor, miracle worker,
longest-living member of his generation,
devoted husband of the late Mary
Browning, beloved father, grandfather,
great-grandfather, brother, and uncle,
of Greenwich, CT, and Palm Beach, FL,
died peacefully at home surrounded by
his family on April 24, 2012. He was an
inspiration to all who knew him. Born
in Manhattan, Robert was the fourth of
six children of Franklin E. Browning
and Lillian Gertrude (English). He
graduated from Trinity School in 1934
and received a BS in theology from
Harvard University in 1938 and an MS
in economics from Yale University in
1939. He joined the venerable investment
bank Allderdyce & Allen before enlisting
in the navy in 1942. Upon his return
from the war, he rejoined the firm. He
became a senior partner in 1964. He had
an extraordinary professional career filled
with accomplishment, but he was most
proud of his philanthropy. He served as
a trustee of Harvard University from
1971 to 1978. He was the president of the
Collegiate School Board of Trustees from
1972 to 1977. He served as governor of
the Society of Mayflower Descendants

in the state of New York and as president of the Sons of the Revolution in the state of New York (1967–1969). He will be best remembered for his sixty-three-year marriage to Mary, who died in 2008. He is survived by his adoring children, Marie (C. Ferguson) Paine of Fairfield, CT; Virginia Doherty of NYC; Robert (Minnie Van der Veldt) Browning Jr. of NYC; and Gregory (Jane Timmings) Browning of Harrison, NY; sixteen grandchildren; and nine great-grandchildren, with another due in July. A Mass of Christian Burial will be offered at the First Presbyterian Church, 55 Stockbridge Street, Rye, NY, on Sunday, March 15 at 11 a.m. In lieu of flowers, friends are strongly encouraged to make donations in his memory to Presbyterian Family Services, 1011 First Ave., New York, NY 10022.

II.

Carole Lee Bingham had the job the moment she walked in—strode in, really—to Stevens' office in the late nineties, announcing herself with her hand out firmly for a shake. For seven years thereafter, she was a crack-bang worker, starting out as his secretary and rising to the position of office manager, though her duties only changed insofar as there was an expansion in the range of small tasks the ever-fastidious, self-reliant, and grindingly precise Stevens would allow her to do. The Binghams were a prominent Georgia family, which, while thoroughly proud, did not appear, from the mosaic pieces thrown out in conversation over years of office proximity, to remain thoroughly rich. Like most Southern girls, Carole Lee's deferential and capable manner made her more attractive than other women. She was curvy with pretty, long brown hair—about 75 percent of a knockout.

Sexual attraction to women in the office place was never an issue for Stevens, who was as straight about straying as he was about punctuation in correspondence, but he wasn't so buttoned down that he didn't recognize Carole Lee's gifts from front to back. He found something about her a bit jaggy—there were little glimpses of craziness—but he cast off these things as imperfections rather than flaws, chipped paint rather than cracks in the foundation. Her frantic phone calls with her mother were about ten yards past the flag, and it seemed bad taste in men had been passed down through the Bingham women to Carole Lee. But she was devoted to Stevens, and he knew she admired him and respected his practice. He was disappointed when, standing where she had stood so many times to ask him how many copies of a lease he needed or to tell him who was on the phone, she revealed she was taking another job involving a vague opportunity for promotion at an investment bank. He was sanguine about it, though; secretaries came and went, like sport coats and golden retrievers. A few would stand out, but all would inevitably go away. They both moved on.

So it was a surprise when she called on a Monday morning three years later and asked if she could stop by.

"Eliot, I am so sorry to bother you..." she said at his doorway.

"Don't be silly," he said, motioning to the chair in front of his desk. "Come in, come in."

Once seated, she smiled and looked around the office. "How's Maribeth? And Alex?"

"Great," he said. "We have a little grandson, you know." He showed her a picture. "He is six months today."

"Oh my God, Eliot, that's wonderful. Congratulations. How precious."

"Yes, it's great, I have to say. Amazing, the simple things. How about you? What's up?"

"Well," she said and let out a big breath. "Speaking of babies…" She gave her lip a little bite. "I'm pregnant."

"That's fabulous," he said. "I didn't know you were—"

"I'm not." She set her hands out in warning. "This will take a minute to explain."

Stevens had not known much about the job Carole Lee had left him for, but it turned out that she had joined Allderdyce and that, by virtue of moving to a big company, her life had become much more social. She moved into an apartment in the West Village and commuted downtown. She filled her time out of the office with trips to the gym and happy hours of margaritas and chips at bars with names like Carramba. "Flirting with all those bankers and lawyers in their yellow ties," she said, and then she wound her way to the present. "His name is Tim. He's married. Very hooked in—his father and uncles and cousins all worked at Allderdyce. His grandfather is, like, a legend there." Stevens noted she had picked up on the mythologizing so prevalent at major companies. It fit her loyal nature. "Tim's office was kitty-corner from me. Over time, well, you know how it goes. He would come and talk to me at my desk nearly every day. Then we got to e-mailing. Flirting, really, is what it was, truth be told. We ended up having an emotional affair for months and months. But eventually he left the bank, and we lost touch."

"An emotional affair?"

"Yes, that's what they call it." She showed an endearing quality at moments like this, down in the nuance.

"Go on."

"He asked me for a drink out of the blue three months ago. He said he'd reached the end with his wife. She is a shrew—we all worked together at the bank. She's, like, this international finance whiz. Her parents brought her here from Russia when she was—I don't know—twelve."

"So he is no longer at the bank?"

"He stayed a broker of some kind. I don't think he's a big deal—it's sort of an excuse to get out of the house. He probably manages his trust fund. They are loaded...*loaded*. Plus, Vera works. She's making bazillions."

Stevens nodded. "They do well at Allderdyce."

"He said he missed me, never stopped thinking about me, and on and on. Oh, goddamn it, it sounds horrible." Carole Lee's hand was on her stomach. "And that we could be together finally—I'm so stupid, I thought he really meant it. We only did it that one night." She saw Stevens' expression and stopped.

"Have you discussed the future?"

She looked away again. "He was fantastic at first. I thought he was actually happy. He was very scared of telling Vera, of course." She took a tissue from an end table. "She's such a witch." She blew her nose. "Eliot, I am so sorry, really. I just don't know who else to talk to."

"Please," he said. "Of course you should come to me." He kept on with his questions. "Has he told her?"

"It was horrible. It turned into a mess as soon as he did. She went crazy. He quit calling me. Then when he did call me, he told me to talk to his lawyer. 'George is great,' he said. As though the lawyer was going to help."

"Is it George Dandridge?"

"Yes." She turned her head sideways. "Wow, how did you know that?"

"There's a small circle in our world. Has George told you to get a lawyer?"

"No."

"Ok." Stevens reached for his pen.

"I thought it better to do whatever Tim asked. I know it sounds stupid. But I had this idea that he would leave her…"

"Never mind. You are here now."

"You don't mind, Eliot? Of course, I will pay you."

"Nonsense…" he said. He looked at his yellow pad in a manner that would show her he was shifting into attorney mode. Her eyes dipped in appreciation. "Let's get started here. I need to know about all of the events specifically and any contact…"

"Yes, ok. You trained me well, Eliot. I have everything he's sent. And the test results."

"You've taken *tests*?"

"Uh-huh. Several. I wouldn't do an amnio, though. Not yet, at least."

"Ok," Stevens said, with a slight hint of anger. He felt from Carole Lee the surge of relief clients give off at the flex of protection, but it was more intense — more internal — than he usually received from the "let's get 'em" of the men of the commercial world. "I know this must be terrible for you. The most important thing…" He pulled back from the bromide — not his specialty and rarely helpful. "How far along are you?"

"She sent me the worst e-mail."

"Who? The wife?"

"I don't even want to show you."

———

Stevens had called George Dandridge and informed him that he would be handling the case by the time Carole Lee forwarded all the correspondence and test results. Since it did no good to attack lawyers like Dandridge — savvy white-shoe creatures who operated according to their own set of rules — Stevens was cordial. Dandridge was suitably surprised and worried: it did not take much to see that the Browning family was in deep, and it was implicit between the lawyers that Dandridge had deepened the amount of shit they were in with *ex parte* communications with Carole Lee. Stevens spent the rest of the day ruminating over the proper moves to make. He felt terrible for Carole Lee's mess but couldn't deny he also had the tingle of leverage.

But even in the state in which Stevens found himself, he was not prepared for the message from Carole Lee when he checked his e-mail before going off to bed:

> Eliot — I had to down a glass of wine to send this to you. I don't even want you to see it. Please don't think less of me. I think knowing this would have to come out is

what almost stopped me from coming to you in the first place. Here it is:

Hi Carole Lee, this is Vera, Tim's wife. That's right, the guy you fucked in order to get pregnant. Congrats! You've succeeded... HOWEVER...what I don't understand is why you think you are in the position to raise a child? You have no job! you are by yourself! and you are obviously too stupid for words as getting pregnant underscores! Why don't you have an abortion and do what is best for this unwanted child? Do you know how horrible this child will feel—knowing how they were conceived and born only because a stupid woman wanted to play Mommy? Do you think my husband actually cares for you? He does feel badly about this child being brought into this world, but he doesn't give a fuck about you—you were a one-night stand. Why can't you do something constructive in your wasted life and dissolve this pregnancy? is this all about money? Because some money can be made available for you—and if you had any sense, that is what you would ask for. Fact: you are DUMB! Fact: you are POOR and don't have a job, career, or any prospects! Fact: no man wants a woman with a bastard child! Fact: you are thirty-five and your looks are not much to begin with! Fact: my husband doesn't give a real damn about you—oh, I forgot you guys have a real bond—you made him ejaculate! GREAT FOR YOU! I've got an idea—maybe you can do that for a living. I take it back—you are good for something. You are not fit to be a mother—not sure if you are fit to be here at all!

Stevens stopped reading. He must have made a noise, because Maribeth was at the threshold of his small office off the front hallway of the brownstone.

"Honey? Are you ok?" she said.

"What?"

"Is it that Trimark thing? I wish you'd either settle that or send it off."

Stevens smiled at her, glad to have her think he was just working on a nasty real-estate closing. "At least all the excitement is making it a good month. Are you going up?"

"Yeah, I'm exhausted. Come watch something with me." She lingered, looking at him closely, until she decided he was ok and turned to leave. "How about *Downton Abbey*?"

"In a minute," he said. "Go get it ready, ok? I'll bring up something for us to share. We still have the ice cream."

"Ooh." She made a little scrunchie face. "Put the Hershey's on it," she said, her thumb and forefinger an inch apart. "Just a little."

He watched Maribeth trudge up the stairs and was transported back to the time when Alex was still in diapers, his little butt working his way up the steps, turning sideways for a rest after each one. Stevens had bought the brownstone a year to the day after hanging his shingle. He had not had a slow moment since, hitting the ground running by subletting from a small firm in the Empire State Building, of all places. Rents were cheap twenty years ago, and Stevens found he could bill 175 hours a month easily among three or four real-estate developers. There was so much more time available to focus on the work when he didn't need to play the politics of making partner. It was a cliché, to be sure, but it was the best thing that had ever happened to him. Stevens thought of his father, as he always did when circumstances stopped him flat, and the kind way he had said, "Son, you don't always need the things you think will fix you. That's why you call a doctor." Stevens wrote an e-mail:

To: gdandridge@csm.com
From: estevens@stevenslawoffice.com
Re: Browning/Bingham
CONFIDENTIAL SETTLEMENT COMMUNICATION

Dear George, as you can see from the hour, I am writing you under abnormal circumstances. Please take a long look at the attached e-mail from Vera Browning to my client. I will spare you the litany of possibilities this presents to you and the Browning family. I will also resist the temptation to scold your client for indolence and outright barbarity. Given our long relationship, out of courtesy to you alone, I will hold off on filing anything with the court until I hear from you — but,

George, do get back to me ASAP. All rights and remedies are hereby reserved in the premises. Eliot.

Within the half hour, a response came:

To: estevens@stevenslawofficeny.com
From: gdandridge@csm.com
Re: Browning/Bingham
CONFIDENTIAL SETTLEMENT COMMUNICATION

Eliot, thank you for the below and for your forbearance. I will call you in the morning to discuss resolving this unfortunate situation before any more harm is inflicted upon either side.

I also want to give you the heads-up that you will be receiving a personal call from Mrs. Browning. As irregular as it sounds (it's safe to say we're both in pretty strange territory), you can take the call, and permission is hereby granted to speak to her directly. She understands the ramifications.

Once again, Eliot, your professionalism and friendship is appreciated in this most troublesome matter. The litigators can get this case soon enough anyway — I'm not sure either of us has a large enough magic wand at this point to accomplish a good result. Oh, for the good old days.

Unless you request otherwise, I will give
her both your office number and your
mobile.
Customary reservation of rights and
settlement privilege.

Thanks again,
George

Stevens smiled as he read. Dandridge had a
smoothness cultivated over a career filled with the
management of rich men's secrets. Cornered and with
devastating evidence of a client gone rogue, George
had played a wily card: familiarity. Against all good
practice, Dandridge had gotten chummier in his writing
("Oh, for the good old days") than protocol allowed.
He was preparing the mood in which he would have to
negotiate the painful settlement that was coming for the
Brownings. It was artful and something a pedestrian
lawyer would have not risked.

Stevens tried to draw a profile of Vera, like a cop
sizing up a pulled-over driver. He spent a little time on
the Internet, and based on that research and Carole
Lee's commentary, he was able to imagine a brilliant,
ball-busting first-generation Russian woman who used
wits and everything else to make it in the lion's den of
Allderdyce. She would have been in the right place
at the right time, coming of age at the firm just as the
Russian and Eastern Bloc economies were opening.
The well-positioned Wall Street firms made billions in
that window of privatization. Vera must have leveraged
her business drive and dazzle into a partnership. At the

time, promoting her would have allowed management to check off two boxes: female and expanding markets. Next, Stevens assumed, came a romantic liaison, followed by a period in which she overpowered the resistance of the blue-blooded Brownings with pure personality. She probably would have contrasted her forcefulness with an unexpectedly endearing subordination to family traditions and somehow found that rare place where the established make a calculated acceptance of outsiders, the way Augusta admitted women. Ultimately there would have been marriage to the malleable Tim — whose parents probably factored in the scion's limitations — and then, after a few children, Vera was set. Big job, big money, big status — a long way from the apartment of two academics on the outskirts of Saint Petersburg.

As Stevens waited for the call the next day, he busied himself with the treble and strife of his daily grind. He reviewed a master commercial lease for CCR violations, spoke to the general counsel of an electrical-engineering firm being acquired by a conglomerate, and dictated a purchase and sale agreement for the physical equipment related to the transaction. All the while he planned his confrontation with the Russian. Should he set her up? She was obviously unhinged — he wondered if he should goad her into saying even more than she'd already written in the e-mail. Or should he play the nice guy and tell her he would help in any way he could to get some sort of peaceful result? He did feel for her after all — her life was being ripped apart.

Line two lit up.

"Eliot Stevens."

"Hello, Mr. Stevens. This is Vera Browning. I believe you are expecting my call." Her voice was professional but shaky and betrayed just slightly that English was not her first language.

"I am. George Dandridge told me you'd be calling and he said it was ok for us to speak directly. What can I do for you?"

"Hah," she said, the sarcasm aggressive through the phone. "I suppose you can do a lot."

"Listen, Mrs. Browning, I have to tell you—this feels like an awkward call…"

"Let's cut through it, ok?"

Stevens went quiet. After a second he said, "Ok. Go ahead."

"Good. Let's begin. Your client is attempting to ruin my life. Let's begin with that. Let's also begin with me telling you it is not something I will allow. She is a stupid slut who manipulated my idiot husband into this situation."

"Mrs. Browning, this conversation isn't going to go very far if you continue to use personal insults. I'm just not going to listen to it."

"Oh please," she said, the hint of accent blending into picked-up New Yorkese. "I can't believe this." A gasket blew. "You know what? *Spare* me, ok? Just fucking *spare* me. You think you can come in here and be some kind of shakedown prick?"

Stevens, as prepared as he thought he was, hesitated. But only for a moment, and then he went into the opening. "Ok, ok. Listen, Mrs. Browning, you need to understand how much money you are spending with each word you say. Do you have *any idea* how much I love what you are saying? Do you?" Stevens paused for effect and then took his tone down a notch. "You may not realize this, but I'm the last reasonable person you are going to talk to. You think things are bad now…wait till I give that e-mail—in which you humiliated yourself, by the way—to a lawyer who would like to do nothing more than attach the assets of you, your husband, your husband's family, and, depending on how clever they want to get, perhaps a bit of Allderdyce's insurance. I'm sure your partners will like that. I'm sure your husband's grandfather will like that." He reduced his tone once more. "Really, this is shocking—a woman of your intelligence putting stuff like this out in writing—you should know better."

"Have you ever had your wife tell you she was pregnant with another man's child, Mr. Stevens?"

"No, and I can't imagine how bad you feel. I know it must be difficult. No one is saying it isn't a hard… Well, you know, this is really a strange conversation to be hav—"

"*How much?*" she screamed. "Tell me how much! Don't try to pretend you're my friend. Don't try to pretend you are doing something right. She has been after money all along—even as a little secretary, she was walking around the office and looking at the married men. You don't know about this bitch. And now you are the man with a hatchet. So again, I say, spare me, Mr. Stevens. You—*you*—need to tell her to do the obvious thing. There is one plain and simple and proper thing to do here, and we all know what it is. This little…*bitch*…is now going to change the life of a family. A big and proud family of many good men. Do you have any idea? I have a five-year-old child. What do I say to her?" She shifted from anger to exasperation. "This is where, honestly, Americans prove what they say in Russia. It is true. Everything done by lawyers." She made a disgusted noise. "You know, you *could* help here. George says you are a good lawyer. You could fix this. This girl—she has no man. She has no father—no one to tell her what to do. You should be that person."

"You're wrong."

"But no, you won't do it. You want the money. You want the money from the family and from the businesses and from me and my husband—and the whole world. So fucking spare me. Tell me how much that piece of shit wants."

Stevens hung up.

III.

During idle lunch hours or when his meetings took him uptown, Stevens liked to wander in the fifties and sixties, just east of the park, looking at buildings. Reliably, he passed by the exclusive social clubs of the City—the Union Club, the Links Club, the Leash Club. When he was starting out at the firm, he thought he might join the Century Club once he made partner. But he gave up the idea when the elevation did not happen. He and Maribeth instead bought a cottage in Columbia County, and he devoted his weekends and the energy he had planned to use in life as a Master of the Universe to the Tennannah Lake Golf and Tennis Club and the Ancramdale Presbyterian Church.

After his call with Vera Browning, Stevens decided to take one of his walks. He took a cab to the park and drifted over to Madison and Park and then Lexington. He went by the Metropolitan with its flags and courtyard manned by a doorman in full battle regalia, a dark blue uniform and hat, maroon capulets, and other fringes. He floated into the midsixties, eventually meandering down Sixty-Sixth Street toward York. It had been a good life, this course he'd pursued. Certainly his mother and father would be proud of him, and he was reasonably sure Alex was as well. The City struck him now as a big grid, the Bronx uptown and the Battery down, two hundred streets divided longways by ten avenues, with tiny parks all around and a big one occupying the middle. There were stories everywhere — in every Korean grocery and Senegalese cardboard rip-off, around every Pakistani cabby and Queens housewife — but in the end each place and each person was a pin on the grid. Obituaries ran every day, on Tuesdays next to the chess; a few of the dead would be there, and everybody else would not.

His cell phone rang. He didn't recognize the number, but as a man trained once and always for the service business, he answered. "Eliot Stevens." There was silence on the other end. "Hello?"

"This is Vera." She was woozy — maybe even drunk. She spoke as though their conversation were just continuing, as though time had stood still while he wandered, as though they were in one of those movie scenes edited to show things happening simultaneously and in gaps, in the streets and in the bars, at intermittent spots throughout the grid.

"Look," he said, "this isn't a good idea. We shouldn't deal directly." He tried to be kind. "It's not…" He heard a sob. A trash truck went by, and he covered the phone. When the noise subsided, she was still crying. "Call George. It's not going to work this way…"

"All I called to say to you, Mr. Stevens…Eliot… whatever," she said, pulling herself together, "is that you can tell your client that I will not bother her again. I'm sorry. Good-bye."

With no other responsible course of action in sight, Stevens turned up the pressure on the Browning family over the next several weeks. He compelled Dandridge to provide a detailed list of all communications with Carole Lee and all test results and medical charges. He also negotiated for Carole Lee a temporary weekly stipend from Tim and procured a written guarantee that all her medical expenses through the birth would be covered. As the process between the lawyers ground on, the fourth and fifth months of Carole Lee's pregnancy passed, and Mother Nature, *Roe v. Wade*, and a vague sort of morality, which grew stronger with time, caused certain options to fall away.

Carole Lee showed up at Stevens' office unannounced on a Tuesday. She brought chocolate-chip cookies, a sign of domesticity Stevens did not remember in the years she had worked for him. As much as he wished she would unburden herself with her mother or her girlfriends, he showed only that he was happy to console her. He did not have his usual clarity on the relationship between his motives and his actions. While she ate one of her own cookies, he realized he had not told Maribeth about Carole Lee's mess because he could not articulate how he was approaching the matter—whether it was as a friend or father or dutifully or responsibly or just because, at bottom, it was a real juicy case against an exposed set of sons of bitches.

"You're not going to believe the latest," Carole Lee said, rolling her eyes. "He called me last night to tell me he's had a change of heart and wants to be with me and raise the baby. He said he just can't take it from Vera anymore. She's torturing him day and night—insulting him in front of the kids and stuff like that."

"What did you say?"

"I tried to be calm about it. I told him he needs to be absolutely certain. I can't go through this again—this seesawing up and down and never knowing."

"Carole Lee, this is not a guy who seems to be in control of his own life. You need to be careful."

"I know." She fingered the sleeve of her sweater. "We sure as hell have learned that, haven't we?" She looked down at the carpet. "The only thing he said that makes me hopeful is he is going to dinner with his grandfather tomorrow night. I swear to God, I think that man is the most important thing in the world to Tim. He admires him so much. You know, he does seem like such an amazing guy. I wish I could just meet him. Just get a chance to talk to him is all. I mean, good lord, I *am* going to have his great-grandson."

Stevens' eyes widened. "You found out?"

"Oh god, I forgot to tell you," she said. She was smiling now—beaming. She moved toward him with her arms outstretched. "Eliot, it's a *boy*."

What Stevens didn't have the heart to tell Carole Lee in his office on chocolate-chip day was that it would be a miracle if Tim did not let her down again before the weekend. And he did so like clockwork, via an email in which he reversed course. Carole Lee let Stevens know with a quick, embarrassed e-mail of her own. Stevens urged her not to get down and to that she was going to be a wonderful mother.

With the clock ticking increasingly loudly, the Brownings' firm relieved Dandridge and brought in its litigators. The tone of the e-mails and communications directed at Stevens became tauter and more threatening. The presence of the court lawyers on the file meant that Stevens really should turn the case over to a litigation firm for Carole Lee, but he dragged his feet because he knew she could not afford it. On the day he decided he could not put it off any longer, he returned from one of his walks uptown to a message: "Robert Browning Sr.'s office called. Wants to have lunch at the Knickerbocker Club tomorrow."

IV.

George Dandridge tells me you don't usually deal with things like this," the old man said as they sat. Browning was taller than Stevens had expected and wore gray slacks, a blue blazer, and deep-brown wing tips. His collar and the skin around his neck were looser than they might once have been, but otherwise he was dapper—well appointed, like a ship in a bottle on the desk of a seasoned man.

"He's right," said Stevens. "Forgive me, but I want to be sure: are you ok with the two of us speaking directly? Without George here?"

Browning waved him off. "Of course, of course." He handed the menu to Stevens, not needing one for himself. "We're the only club in New York still making an oyster stew, I believe."

"Yes, I've been here a few times," Stevens said. They were in the men's dining room on the second floor overlooking the east side of the park from Sixty-Second Street.

"At eighty-nine, Mr. Stevens, I am granting myself the liberty to speak without my lawyers. No offense, but it is faster this way."

Stevens nodded. "None taken."

The waiter appeared with glasses of water and bread and butter. In his white jacket and black bowtie, the short man had obviously been at the club for many years. Browning said, "How is it today, O'Hara? Are we keeping this place straight?"

"Yes, sir, Mr. Browning," he said.

The old man ordered the dover sole, peas, and shoestring potatoes. Stevens said he would have the same.

Browning got right to the point. "How long have you known the woman?"

"Quite some time," said Stevens. "She was my secretary for seven years, actually."

"You have your own shop?" Browning asked. His eyes were full of fluid and sharp like blue yolks of runny eggs. "You worked with George?"

"Yes. But I left the firm twenty years ago."

"This sort of case is not really up your alley, is it? You usually handle commercial matters, I suspect?"

"Well, that's right. But I do a lot of things. Corporate and real estate, mostly. George and I run into each other quite often."

"Yes, he's told me all about you. I take it, then, you are handling this as a favor?"

"Are you asking me whether Carole Lee is paying me, Mr. Browning?"

"Certainly not." The old man spread his napkin, elegantly refusing to be gainsaid. "I am asking you if you are representing this girl—who is claiming to be pregnant with my grandson's child—as a personal friend." He paused. "And, I suppose, I am asking if the letters you've sent George Dandridge regarding the pregnancy were sent as a favor for a friend or whether they have been sent at an arm's length. I'd like to know this, Stevens—that's all. I wouldn't expect it to be a controversial question."

"Mr. Browning, with all due respect, your grandson is the father of the child. George Dandridge is a very good lawyer, and he and—by extension—your family have put my client through quite a bit of strife. She has taken blood tests and ultrasounds. Carole Lee gave a sworn statement and produced hotel receipts. She had complied with everything—done *everything* your people asked—*before* she even contacted me." He looked at Browning and, like a doctor bearing bad news, said, "There is no question of paternity, Mr. Browning, and I think you know that."

"What do you want?" asked the old man.

"What are you offering?"

"No, I asked you what *you* want."

"Sir?"

"Stevens," said Browning, "don't toy with me and don't threaten me. You are not in a position to threaten me."

"You have that wrong, Mr. Browning. You're not in a position to tell me not to threaten you."

Browning stared back at him for a long moment as though he were thinking through an equation. Then he relaxed his face. O'Hara interrupted with their food, and they did not speak until he had gone away. "Eliot…" he said and then stopped. "May I call you Eliot?"

"Of course."

"Eliot, I have a question for you: did you take this situation on for some kind of reason? Something inside of you?"

Stevens kept his hands folded on the table. "I don't follow."

"Listen," said Browning, "I don't know what you know about me, but I assume you have done your research. You should consider that I've done mine as well."

"I think you are missing the point, Mr. Browning."

"Oh no, I don't think I am at all." The old man sat back but at the same time reached for his water glass, which he continued to hold throughout the conversation without drinking, as though he needed it to anchor him. His voice turned fatherly. "Look, I know what happened with you at the Mason firm, not making partner. Do you carry that around? All that weight of expectation for years and then all of a sudden having to grab your boots and set your sights more realistically? To move on from it to earn a living for your family? It is a hell of a thing to carry, you know. I admire a man who can do that."

"That was a long time ago," said Stevens. "I hardly think about it."

"That's not what I see." Browning hunched in. "Listen, are we talking like grown men? If your experience in life has been marked with a disappointment like that, take an old man's word for it that it's better to look at the other side. If not making partner at the firm is even partly responsible for your success, well, you should be grateful to it."

"I don't know how we got off on this. This is not about me. This is about your son's obliga—"

Browning made a dismissive sound. "Please stop it, Eliot. This girl worked for you for seven years. You did not get to where you are by not being able to recognize a goldiggger when you see one."

In the rear of the room, a busboy dropped a plate on the black-and-white marbled floor, sending a smash through the club. Neither man flinched.

Browning shook his head. "No, I am not willing to believe that...that you cannot see through her." He looked down at his water glass and kept his eyes there. "What I *am* inclined to believe, though, is that once this came into your sights, you did not take it on for the money." Stevens listened. "I think you took it on because you saw my name. And you saw—you see now—a chance to strike justice. I think you are out for something." He tilted his head down and cut his fish. As he took a bite, he said, "Am I right?" The question stayed in the air for a beat before the old man made a swatting motion with his hand. "Never mind. You don't have to answer. But it is not justice, Eliot. I want you to know that." Browning put a lifetime of practice with persuasion into what he was saying now. "It's not just. Not right. And in the end that will not benefit you. Or your client. Or the child."

Stevens said, "Believe what you want."

Browning put down his fork and wiped his mouth. "Look, my grandson made a mistake. A terrible mistake that has created a terrible problem that we now have to face and do our best to solve consistently with our consciences and the good Lord." Stevens thought he saw Browning's hand shake — an almost-imperceptible tremor. "Now, I am quite certain that this young woman will trust and follow your advice. So, really, *you*, Eliot, are the principal in this discussion, and *you* will make a decision based upon your own personal prejudices." Browning let go of the drinking glass and returned his arm to his lap. "When there is a mistake, I move swiftly to correct it. I am not interested in fighting with you or with this girl. What should come as no surprise is that I do not want any damage done to my family or to its name. You and I need to come to an understanding. There is a child involved — a human life. A life that will last, God willing, for many years after you and I are gone. There is nothing to argue about here. From this point on, I am personally guaranteeing you things will be looked after."

Stevens felt the opening Browning was giving him click like a door unlocking. The waiter interrupted again to check on their food, and the men nodded him away. When he was out of earshot, Stevens outlined a financial arrangement, beginning with a large sum of money to be transferred to Carole Lee. It would ostensibly be for medical expenses but well in excess of any realistic estimate of such needs, a point that Stevens artfully avoided making directly to the old man, who nodded quietly. After covering the payment to Carole Lee, Stevens proposed that a trust be established for the child and enumerated another healthy—this time monthly—sum the family would be required to pay. Browning swiftly agreed to the child-support payment and added that, in fact, the financial settlement as a whole was acceptable. He even went so far as to give Stevens a compliment on the deal, like an experienced carpenter judging a well-made table. Browning said his only request in return was that Carole Lee sign a confidentiality agreement. Stevens expected as much. "Mr. Browning," he said, "Carole Lee has no intention of embarrassing your grandson or your family."

Browning nodded, satisfied. He called for the waiter and asked Stevens, "Do you have time for a cup of coffee?"

Stevens, aware he had just leveraged a very wealthy man, was experienced enough in the denouements of negotiations to maintain his composure throughout moments like this. Sometimes it was ironing out paperwork; other times it was discussing the timing of payments. He had taught himself to exit gracefully and not rub it in. "Sure," he said.

"Do you take anything with it?"

"Just a little milk."

To O'Hara, Browning said, "Two cups of old-fashioned coffee, one black and one with cream. And bring us a piece of that cheesecake."

"Your cordial, as well?" said the waiter.

Browning smiled at Stevens, who was happy to once again play the role of the lunch guest. "A habit adopted from my father when he was alive, I'm afraid." The old man seemed tired.

"Do you spend much time in the city anymore?" Stevens asked.

"A few times a month I come in. These days I only get in for my work on the board at Saint Matthew's."

"You've done so much there."

"Why, thank you, Elliot. That's quite kind of you. Do you know the church?"

"Of course," said Stevens. "We are at Old First, but I've been many times. Many weddings."

"That's better than many funerals."

"Yes, to be sure."

The coffee and dessert arrived along with Browning's little drink. Stevens figured it was probably cognac. Browning swirled it and sipped. Stevens thought about the style with which he did it—it was an efficient and brief motion. In the hands of another man, another type, it would be an affectation, an air. But it fit the old man perfectly. Stevens could see all the generations of Brownings sipping cognac after lunch at polished tables under painted ceilings. It was a touch off-center in the stuffy club, a touch Scotch-Irish, giving a hint of their individuality within their elite world, like all families in such circumstances: their clan being utterly unique to their own minds, while the rest of the population wouldn't see a whit of difference in any of the room's denizens at any point in the last fifty years. The drinking of the cordial showed—more than any kind of conformity—Browning's complete comfort.

"You have to try this," he said, dipping his fork into the cheesecake. Stevens did so, made a suitably surprised face, and told Browning that it was, in fact, delicious. "Speaking of Saint Matthew's," Browning said, "I must tell you that the annex is a tremendous resource. It is entirely your business, of course, but I am happy to assist."

Stevens nodded, pretending to know what Browning was talking about. He assumed the old man was weary and, with the cognac, trailing off a bit. He thought suddenly and inexplicably of his own father. "I know the church covers many things."

"Yes, the social services staff handles sensitive matters like these terribly well. You know, I can remember when the annex got started forty years ago."

"These matters?"

"Yes. The adoptions. They find wonderful homes — reputable families who have not been blessed with children."

Stevens closed his eyes and sought the same reservoir of control that allowed him to stay calm in victory. "Mr. Browning, you don't seem to understand. Carole Lee is going to keep the child — the boy. That is what the trust is for."

"Oh no, no," said Browning, his eyebrows arched. "I thought it was understood…She has to give the baby up. We are not having her raise my grandson's child. I'm surprised you even…"

The blood ran out of Stevens' face. The room, the club, and the occasional fully male sound of wood chairs jerking across marble all conspired to add to his disbelief. He had an impulse to backhand the drinking glass off the table and envisioned ice and water spraying the old man's suit. He got hold of himself. "You are not going to be able to do that, Mr. Browning," he said. "If you go down that road, you will only cause yourself and your family embarrassment. I can't tell you what to do —

you can listen to me or not listen to me — I don't really care. I'm just her lawyer. But you can't fix this one. Not even you. There is a child. Your grandson is that child's father. She will keep the baby, and he is responsible for helping her. The law is the law." Stevens folded his napkin, set it on the table, and stood. "I'm happy to let a judge decide all of this from here. Thank you for lunch." Stevens walked downstairs and out of the club. It was the last he ever saw of Robert Browning Sr.

V.

Maribeth made a habit of collecting the Christmas and holiday cards in a large Mexican ceramic bowl. That way Stevens did not have to peck away at three or four sets of matching sweaters with smiling faces in the daily mail or pay attention to the mass preprinted corporate throwaways, which seemed like soon-to-be remnants of a distant age, like the well-written letters opened by Lord Grantham on *Downton Abbey*. Stevens liked to wait for Christmas Eve, and then, as Maribeth was cooking and Alex and Jen sat in the kitchen with wine glasses, he would pour himself his one scotch of the winter, put Nicholas on his lap, and go through the cards, sifting slowly through the whole accumulation, showing his grandson the colors and pictures while he cataloged the growing offspring of neighbors and clients and relatives. He and Maribeth had a private contest in which they each tried to discover the craziest card, so he kept his eyes peeled for the one — there was always one — that signaled a card maker for whom the stitching had come off the ball. The winner usually came from an overstressed woman with teenagers who was chucking in the towel by sending something reckless, the housewife version of not showing up in court. It might be a black card with red block letters reading *Merry Christmas* and nothing else — not even signatures. Or, in the other direction, it might be a themeless, titleless, multiphoto, rococo monstrosity so blazed up with braces, soccer uniforms, and formless-faced infants that one could almost see its author drunk with the power of new corner-cutting software.

He had come to look forward to this annual half hour now that Nicholas was five. It had settled the way quirky family customs do, with Maribeth and Alex and Jen bending toward its occurrence at the appointed time. It was becoming, all in all, a nice time of life for Stevens. "A grandson on your lap will do that," he thought to himself. Nicholas fished in the bowl and handed Stevens a dark-red card. The front cover said *Happy Holidays!*

"What do we have here, buddy boy?" Stevens opened it. Under the lettering was a large photo of a little girl, probably three years old, with a giant smile that reached out and snatched the heart. She was in a puffy red dress with a blue belt and black-and-white saddle shoes. The composition of the card — its background, the letters, and the dress — was confident and happy. "Adorable," Stevens said out loud, which was not like him — perhaps he was feeling the scotch a little. He lingered on the child's face and found he was taken in by something: a sparkle or maybe just the color and the openness of the eyes. He had a remote feeling of recognition, something he couldn't quite put his finger on. His gaze trailed over to the message, which read, *Every good gift and every perfect gift is from above. James 1:17. Much Love This Christmas from Carole Lee and Scarlett Lee.*

Beneath the printing was a handwritten note: *Eliot and Family—sending you warm wishes and lots and lots of love. May all your dreams come true. xxx.*

"Maribeth, come look at this," he said in a voice loud enough to reach the kitchen.

Stevens thought back to Robert Browning Sr.'s death notice. He remembered something about great-grandchildren, and he wondered now how the issue had been treated by the people who submitted it to the *Times*, what their thoughts and calculations must have been. Nicholas reached for the card to put it in the pile of ones that had already been reviewed, but Stevens held it back gently. "Wait a second, kiddo," he said. "Let me show this one to Nana."

White Man's Problems

The battlefield at Fredericksburg was smaller than Doug Hansall expected, encroached by real-estate development below The Sunken Road, the high ground from which the Confederates blew away a good chunk of the Union Army. "Just drop me off here," Hansall said to the limo driver. He handed the guy a twenty and wheeled his bag toward a busman overwhelming the driver's seat of a tour bus in the Visitor's Center parking lot.

"Do you have a bunch of California kids?" Hansall asked.

The fat man jerked a finger backward, toward the battlefield. "Out there." Sensing the driver was acting as the group member and treating Hansall as the outsider, Hansall thought he should explain, "I'm catching up with them. You with us all week?"

"Yup."

"Great. You can put my bag in with the others."

Uphill on the grassy incline, he saw a schoolteacher standing next to a tour guide who was dressed like a state trooper. Hansall's son, Will, was seated Indian-style with the rest of the Webster Elementary fifth grade, listening to the trooper's talk. "Unlike the Union Army, who couldn't seem to keep a general," said

the guide, "the South was blessed with leadership..."
Hansall circled the semicircle of kids to give Will a
hug. The weight of connection and filial duty not yet
outbalanced by embarrassment at what the world
might see, the eleven-year-old boy greeted him with a
quick kiss.

Hansall stood back among the other chaperones,
parents he knew vaguely from drop-offs on Thursday
mornings and every-other-weekend stints in the
bleachers at Little League and soccer. A woman he
recognized from the school approached. It was Will's
teacher, a girl in her midtwenties.

"Hey, you made it," she said.

"Yes, hi. I hope my office got you the message that I
had to go to New York."

"Oh sure." She gave him a slap on the arm. "We all
know you didn't want to fly in coach." A woman standing
nearby gave a sideways smile.

"No, no," he said. "Just couldn't get out of it. How
was the flight?"

"Will was fine," she said. "I think they are all tired.
We had to be at the airport at *four*, you know." She
waved at the other adults. "I know *we're* all tired." The
mom gave another smile; she had a sweeter face than the
botoxed women he normally saw at the school. A little
horsey, but with kind eyes. The teacher said, "Will you
please just check in with your guys?"

He looked at the sea of kids. "Remind me, which
ones are mine?"

She pointed to four boys for whom he had
preassigned responsibility. "You have Will, Jobie,
Declan, and Harry." Declan and Harry he knew for

years, but Jobie was new to him. He was an Asian, maybe Vietnamese.

"Let's walk down the road," said the tour guide trooper. "There is an authentic section of the wall at the end. It might be hard to believe now, but this ground you are walking was the site of some of the most awful killing in our history. It's a great place to start a trip."

The kids rose and followed and the adults moved with them. Hansall said hello to Declan and Harry, who were a lot like Will: polite at first bite, but beginning to enjoy being far away from their parents. The teacher said to Jobie, who was trailing the other boys, "Come here and say hello to Mr. Hansall."

Jobie looked at him. His eyes were respectful, his manner deferential, but not obsequious. Fifth graders on this trip, like Will, Hansall suddenly felt, were at the edge between the sweetness of childhood and the bored, gawky disposition of teenagers. But Jobie challenged this assumption, and the contrast sent a pang through Hansall about his own child. Jobie seemed younger, more innocent. He had parts of Will that were gone for good.

The teacher produced a small envelope from her bag and presented it to Hansall. Inside was a clip of bills; she held onto it for an extra second for emphasis. "This is Jobie's money. His mom would like you to hold it for him. Jobie is going to ask you for it whenever he wants to buy something, right, Jobie?"

The kid nodded.

"Ok," said Hansall. "How much are we starting with?"

"One hundred and fifty-three dollars," Jobie said.

"All right, man. You come to me when you want something." Hansall tousled his black hair.

Jobie ran back to the pack, and Hansall and the teacher continued at the rear of the group as it made its way alongside the famous stone wall. He looked downhill to the right, from the position where Confederate soldiers shot down the waves of approaching Yankees.

"You have to use your imagination," said the trooper, now next to him. "The houses kind of run up on us here."

Two hundred and fifty yards from the wall was a housing development. Blacktop surrounded the homes, which were arranged in four lines running away from where the tour group stood. The structures were middling; not the kind of fancy development for middle managers and accountants seen in the suburbs, but neither were they shitholes with clotheslines and junk cars in the front yards. The trooper said, "You have to picture the Union soldiers coming up from two miles away. Coming and coming, all the while getting massacred by the Southern guns behind this wall."

"Pretty stupid," replied Hansall to no one in particular.

The woman walked past and made eye contact again, but was soon distracted by a girl, her daughter, Hansall assumed, who reached up to whisper to her mom's ear. They glanced at him while she spoke.

Will did not sit next to Hansall on the bus, preferring to join Declan in a seat in the back near the bathroom, which Mrs. Coyle, the other schoolteacher on the trip and chief disciplinarian, had admonished the kids not to use. She had a chipmunk's cheeks and a helmet of caramel and gray hair. Hansall chose a seat about four rows deep—not back with the kids, but not in the front

with Mrs. Coyle, her younger colleague, and a smattering
of mothers, all yapping and eating snack foods.

"I'm Linda," said the woman, now seated across from
him. "I guess you're the only dad." He introduced himself
and then they smiled for a moment, staring ahead.

Finally, he said, "How long you in for?"

"Oh, it's not that bad," she said with a wave. "C'mon,
we'll have fun."

"Just kidding. You have a daughter?"

"Yes. Rebecca."

"Wait, I know Rebecca." A lean black-haired thing
with worrisome teeth, he recalled. "We were in third
grade together, right?"

"Right. We never really met."

"Yeah, that was a crazy time for me. I wasn't around
too much."

Hansall knew Linda knew why. His thoughts
returned to when it had all gone down. The affair, the
discovery of the affair, the pregnancy, the separation,
and the divorce. The conversation with Will about living
apart. The conversation with Will about having a new
baby sister. The conversation with Will about having
a new baby sister who was going to live in New York,
where Hansall would have to be a lot.

"Do you know Will's mom?" he said.

"Not really. We say hi, but we've never really spent
much time together." She held her hand to the side of
her mouth in mock secrecy. "You know. I have a *girl*."

"Oooh, Yeah. Right. *Boys and Girls*. Sheesh."

The conversation stalled and Linda went back
to her book. He looked out the window as they drove

toward Williamsburg, where they would spend the next two nights. He then moved to Linda's side of the aisle. She lowered her book to talk. "Is your husband happy to have the house to himself?" Hansall asked.

"I'm divorced, too," she said, seeming eager to surprise him. "Two years." She gave a forced smile. "Club D."

Her confession surrounded him like warm water; it was like she had told him that she, too, had been touched in a bad place. "What do you do for work?"

"Real-estate broker. You?"

"Lawyer."

———

Mrs. Coyle left them on the bus while she strode ashore of the lobby of the Williamsburg Marriot like a GI hitting Normandy Beach. Upon her return, she read off names and handed the adults room keys. The kids without parent chaperones were assigned three to a room, while the grownups were given doubles to share with their own offspring.

Will immediately objected to the arrangement. This petition was joined in by Declan and Harry. Hansall made a quick calculation of the risks involved in contending with Mrs. Coyle versus making Will happy and getting his own room. His better angel wanted to be close with his son, to bond over teeth brushing and shower taking; his bad angel wanted to be left alone, to sleep deeply and without obligation in the hotel sheets. The trump factor, though, was that he recognized why Will wanted to be in a cheesy Marriott with other kids, where they could jump on the beds and sleep on the floor and ring

the girls' doorbells and run back into their room
He cut the corner by getting permission for the room
charges from the young teacher instead of Mrs. Coyle,
who was busy putting down a clamor among the girls.

He led the way down the long Marriott hallway
until the boys, reading the signs faster than he, sprinted
down to 406. Hansall got them inside and surveyed the
grounds as sleeping arrangements were made. Then
he went to his room, 412, took the comforter and half
the pillows, and brought them back to 406. Harry and
Declan assembled a pillow/blanket pod between the two
beds, where Will, as last man in, would sleep.

"Do you have my money?" Jobie said.

Hansall hit his pant leg. "Right here."

The boys were told to brush their teeth and get
to sleep, but Hansall knew and they knew that his
instructions were toothless business. Hansall didn't
care. He had discharged his duty. *Let them have some
fun.* The teachers would come down on them when need
be. He went to his room.

His cell phone rang as he walked over the threshold.

It was Johanna. "How is he?" she said.

"He's fine. He's asleep."

"How are Dana and Marjorie?"

"Who are Dana and Marjorie?"

"The teachers. Marjorie is the older one. Dana is the
one you'll be hitting on."

"They're fine."

"Do they all know you lied about the New York trip
so you didn't have to ride in coach?"

"As a matter of fact, I think they do. I think they
hate me. I think they all hate me, so you'll be happy."

She exhaled, "I told you, don't fuck this up. I never should have let this happen."

He heard her shake her head. The ability to hear her actions was actually something he acquired long ago, during the earliest years of their relationship, when arguments were the normal arguments of two people invested with each other. Arguments that people know they have to end. But now the tone had changed, the investment was gone. The fights were the fuel which got them through the day. They were adversaries. Not just in matters of the heart; not just betrayal and bonds broken. They were actual litigants now that she was moving to reduce his custody rights and increase his support. His financial deposition was in three weeks.

"Ok, let's not do this," he said.

"No one is fooled, just so you know. Everyone knows what you're doing."

"Can I go now?"

"Make sure he calls me in the morning."

Fifteen minutes later Hansall was in bed. The room quality was beneath his low expectations. No minibar, no nothing. The only extravagance was a small coffee maker and the accoutrements for a one-cup morning pop, complete with a spongy to-go cup and powdered dairy packets.

Thankfully, the Marriott's no-frills attitude did not extend to the world of pay-per-view movies. With a product loyalty he could never muster in the supermarket when trying to pick a medium hot salsa or organic oatmeal, Hansall scrolled past the "Still in Theaters" and "Best of TV" and went right to "Adults Only." He navigated past the traditional porn offerings

(*Driving Miss Daisy Crazy*) and attendant seals of approval (*AVN Rated Top Sex Scene of 2008*) to the Real Amateurs section. He was turned on by the images of real people being caught on camera having real sex, even when he knew they were probably not so amateur. Finding really good amateur porn was difficult: his special area of porno connoisseurship. He didn't go around buying the stuff. But when he found himself in a hotel room, or occasionally when drifting on the Internet late at night—that is, at those times when porn presented itself—he liked the amateurs.

He especially liked auditions. This usually involved a guy behind the camera, the surrogate narrator, the embodiment of "you" in the fantasy, who conned young girls into sitting on a couch and submitted themselves to an interview which eventually led to taking their clothes off and performing sex acts with the anonymous guy behind the camera. The sex was titillating, but the mental exercise of discerning the level of truth to the setup was the real trick to it. It was easy to make the girls seem inexperienced, but the real accomplishment was to make the corruption seem true. Like the finest jazz or a revelatory Bordeaux, it was layered complexity that set off a fine piece of audition porn.

Hansall didn't reflect on it. He knew it was not a problem, the way excessive drinking or gambling can be. He wasn't like that; addictions didn't plague him. But as with the seemingly hundreds of other consumer choices a normal American faces in a day or week or lifetime — *what your signature soft drink is, or what do you think about electric cars, recycling, Guantanamo, do you wear the size that's smaller or the one that's more comfortable, even if it is XL?*—he thought it through in great detail, punishing himself for an instant, processing a matrix of factors such as title, descriptions, third-party endorsements. He knew the girls on the promo page were never in the video itself, yet he couldn't help imagining he was moments away from seeing them with dicks in their mouths. Was there any kind of process which protected the porn consumer, he wondered, against false advertising like this? He selected *Amateur Screen Test*.

The TV screen displayed a ticking clock with the caption, "One moment please, your selection is starting." But after three minutes Hansall realized it wasn't clicking over. He went to the Main Menu and began the process again. This time the ticking clock remained on digital hold, promising him what he wanted but not actually giving it to him.

He called the front desk.

"I can't get a movie," he said to the desk clerk.

"Let me take a look," the girl said. After a moment, she came back. "Movie system is on, don't know what the problem is."

"That's weird," Hansall said.

"Unless you're trying to get something that's child protected. Hold on." She left the line and returned. "Yeah, your room is child protected. Are you trying to get an adult film, sir?"

He froze.

"It says here this block of rooms is child protected. Are you with a school group?"

"No, I was trying to get something else. Forget it. I was really just calling for a wake-up call. Can you put me down for six thirty?"

"You're already set for a wake-up call at six a.m., sir."

"Well, make it six thirty."

"Ok, fine."

He turned the light off and tried to sleep. As his eyes adjusted to the darkness, he looked at the curtains above the radiator in front of the window. They were dark and polyester, a sort of unidentifiable color that did not quite match the carpet and the paint. What makes a hotel room cheap? Is it simply the finishes, the quality of the sheets and drapes, the infrequency of the paint jobs? Or is it more the architecture of the building, the size of the rooms, the way the edifice is set up? That's it, he thought; a hotel room is cheap long before they fill it with shitty building-grade sinks, faucets, and sheer shades hung inside awful curtains. Bad hotel rooms are conceived in mediocrity. They are not meant to be great.

No one is fooled, just so you know. Johanna was saying he was only on the trip to bolster his defense against her motion to reduce his visitation rights. His lawyer advised him to do as much with Will as possible while they were battling it out, and Hansall had moved his schedule around to make the DC trip. He had sacrificed a week in Hawaii, his first real vacation since the mess with Francesca concluded with her relocation with the baby to New York. He had a moment of gratitude that a baby didn't require a phone call late at night. The Ambien was not working. Tonight was extra hard, he reasoned, and he went to the bathroom and popped another. He was sure he could score one or two later in the week from one of the moms. He sat on the edge of the bed and looked at the curtains again. Why was he even fighting for Will? Did he really want to be with him, or was it the appearance of being an involved father he was after? You couldn't possibly not fight a motion to reduce involvement with a child. To give in was to give up, even if a part of him was thrilled at the prospect of one fewer day per week taken up with mothers, teachers, kids, and fathers who knew what he had done.

———

By 9:30 a.m., the group stood in the intersection of the two main dirt roads of their destination, the Colonial Village of Williamsburg. Mrs. Coyle was previewing the day.

"Ok, Websters, we have a lot to do. This is busy, busy, busy. No lollygagging, you have to stay with me. We'll be here until four thirty. The shoppes and the crafts people are one hundred percent authentic to colonial times. You could really spend a week here, and we're trying to do it in a day, so stay focused."

Linda was standing next to him, just behind Rebecca and with her arms draped on the little girl's shoulders. Hansall moved to get Linda's attention, acting as though he needed to tell her something important. She leaned in. "I think," he whispered, "I would prefer to spend the next eight hours in prison. You know, a jail. I'm not sure if I'd take federal prison. It's a close call."

She closed her eyes and shook her head from side to side, smile cracking. "Stop it."

He moved in for more. "This is a trip my grandmother would take. I *hate* this."

"*Stop...*"

"Craftsmen. Think about it. All day with the crafts of the seventeenth century."

She talked out of the side of her mouth out of respect for Mrs. Coyle's lecture. "You're not interested at all?"

"No. It's a hundred and ten out here. I've already sweated through my clothes. Don't get too close."

"Oh c'mon, it's fun," Linda said. "You're a big baby." She looked up at him. "A very big baby. How tall are you anyway?"

"Not important. Ok, six three."

She giggled. "Yeah, right. You're not *that* big."

"Back to this: I'd rather stick pins in my eyes."

Twenty minutes later they were by a brickmaking site, complete with a large kiln and work tables, where a rugged man with a ponytail like Mel Gibson wore in that Revolutionary War movie was yelling, "Are we making bricks today? What do you think?" He glowered at the kids. When no answer came, he said, "Of course we're not making bricks today. When do you make bricks?"

"In the summer," Mrs. Coyle shouted.

"That's right. And *why* do you make bricks in the summer?"

Hansall looked at his shoes and thought, *it sure fucking feels like summer.*

The mason kept shouting. "You make bricks in the summer because that's when the clay is *dry*." His tone betrayed his contempt for their lack of historical knowledge. Hansall noted Mrs. Coyle, decked out in black polyester pants and a red shirt, nodding in approval. Hansall felt his hatred for her flair up into his nostrils.

The berating continued as the group moved throughout the points of interest. The silversmith was angry they didn't know the value of a shilling; the apothecary threatened to bleed them. The roaming street actors had weird tics, and Hansall occupied himself trying to determine whether these were attributable to the acting. The basket maker had a little cry in her voice. *Was she trying to sound colonial?* The blacksmith was a big man, much less articulate than the other performers. *Was he cast as the kind of strong, silent, and ruddy fellow who would shoe horses? Or was he just the only guy in the area who fit the part? How deep did these things go?*

Mrs. Coyle became excited shortly before lunchtime when she saw Patrick Henry, in search of clots of children to whom he could give rousing speeches. After a ten-minute roadside rant, during which sweat dripped in ball-bearing-sized droplets from his face, the group moved to lunch at Wetherburn's Tavern. The kids were directed to a long table. The air smelled of french fries.

Hansall sat in a chair next to Linda at the grownup table. Waitresses in wench costumes hustled around, pouring water and Coca-Cola from plastic pitchers. "Choice of chicken fingers or Caesar salad with chicken," the wench said. She was older, certainly past retirement age, as were most of the people who worked in the town. She was especially ugly, Hansall thought. He considered what these wenches were paid and whether they had a union, and if so, what freak show those union meetings must have been.

"Ye olde chicken fingers?" he said, looking at Linda for a laugh.

The wench was not amused. "Never heard that one before."

All six adults ordered the Caesars. Miss Barlow asked for a pitcher of Diet Coke, and when the waitress returned, the group held their plastic drink cups up like Dickensian children asking for more.

"Can I get some water, also?" Hansall said after his cup was full. It was something he'd asked in restaurants a million times before, not so much a request as an instruction. He turned to Linda, and said, "You know, I'm not even so sure how realistic any of this is."

The old wench said back to him, "I just gave you Diet." She pointed at his plastic cup.

"Yes, and I would like a glass of water, too." He tried to walk it back. "Please."

Once he was satisfied the wench was complying with his wishes, he returned his attention to Linda. "*I just gave you Diet*. Can you believe she just said that?"

"I used to be disgusted, now I try to be amused."

Hansall laughed in relief. The rest of the women did not make eye contact with him. It was, by now, a familiar feeling.

"Well, it is hot, huh?" Linda finally said to the table.

The rest of the ladies nodded and went back to their conversations. Mrs. Coyle rose and headed toward the kids' table, her instinct for misconduct triggered like a clock-radio alarm in the morning.

"You were saying?" Linda said.

"Huh?" Hansall said.

"You were saying you don't think this is realistic?"

"Well, no," he said. "It's just, with the plastic and the french fries, and the pretend Patrick Henry...you know. Maybe it's just that I was a history major and it bugs my sense of something."

"I was a history major, too," she said, her voice on the upswing.

"Really, where did you go?"

"Just to Fullerton," she said. "But I love history."

He waited for her to ask him where he went to school, but she didn't. He took it for insecurity, that she was self-conscious about her education.

"What did you specialize in?" he said.

"We did a lot of American History—that's why this is so exciting to me. I've never been back here."

———

The afternoon ended with an elaborate staged argument in the public square about the free rights of Englishmen, resulting in an almost-lynching of a tavern dweller who had cursed the Crown. Hansall remembered he had not put sunblock on Will. At four forty-five they made their way toward the exit, which was, of course, by the Gift Shoppe. The teachers granted everyone fifteen minutes to search for souvenirs.

It was a modern store, fresh with beige floor, beige shelves, and beige lighting. Pencils, snow globes, and T-shirts were intermixed with specialty calendars with photographs of *The Beautiful Colonial Village of Williamsburg at Night*, silver spoons, printed china, stuffed bears with hats reading *Grandma and I love Williamsburg*. Will wanted to buy an authentic colonial pipe with a stem reaching eighteen inches, and after a minor protest, Hansall relented. Will also made him try on, and then insisted he buy, a three-cornered hat. Declan and Harry each chose a paperweight. As Hansall stood in the checkout line with the boys, Jobie tugged at his shirt.

"Can I have my money?"

"Well, show me what you want to buy," said Hansall.

"I need ninety-five dollars."

"Whoa, whoa. Ninety-five dollars? What's ninety-five dollars?"

Jobie produced a box set of fifteen commemorative handcrafted silver spoons, the choice of a real Williamsburg devotee.

"Hey, no. C'mon, man. That's too much, these are too much."

Jobie looked up at him in protest.

"Dude, that would be spending most of your money. You have to save some of it."

"Yeah, but…"

"What?"

"It's my money." Jobie said it with firmness. Hansall felt a wave of accusation, as though he were the boss man withholding a miner's wages at the company store. Jobie's big black eyes were on him. His bangs were chopped severely, giving the appearance of a child who called for no ceremony, no grand expense. *It's my money.* The kid was right about that. Hansall was tempted to give Jobie the glassine bag and tell him to go nuts. It *was* his fucking money, after all. Hansall did the math quickly in his head. If he bought the spoons, how much would be—was there sales tax? Wait, wasn't this whole Revolutionary War business about tax anyway? He concluded the kid would have about forty-five bucks left. That could be enough for the rest of the trip.

Mrs. Coyle was suddenly next to them. "What's the problem?" she said.

"Jobie wants to buy these spoons. They're ninety-five bucks. I told him they're too expensive."

Mrs. Coyle took over. "Jobie, that's too much. You won't have enough money left, honey. Go find something else." The boy turned to go, but not before shooting back a final glance.

"You have to just say no," Mrs. Coyle said after Jobie walked off. "They're idiots sometimes." She gave Hansall a smile. "But they're cute."

After another night battle with the green drapes and the fading darkness, Hansall faced the Marriott's morning buffet. His three boys were already eating their bacon-only breakfast when he arrived at the table. A waitress dropped off coffee and orange juice, much as a postal worker drops off the mail. The pans over the Bunsen burners at the buffet table held piles of sausage, scrambled eggs, and other familiar breakfast fare. Having grown up in Connecticut, he associated grits with being somewhere against his will. Hansall hated Texas, Florida, and Atlanta, was not excited by Nashville, and did not see the wonder of Charleston.

After breakfast, Hansall squeezed in next to Will, who was against the window in the midbus range he preferred. Linda sat a row in front of them, her daughter pressed up against the glass. Hansall looked at Will, who was strapped into earphones and watching his iPhone. On the screen, a group of rappers gesticulated at the camera. The lead singer smiled, displaying a solid gold grill. All over the bus, kids were riveted by LED screens. Hansall's phone buzzed.

"Put him on," said Johanna.

"Here. It's your mom."

He handed the phone to Will, who removed his headphones, smiled, and said, "Hi, Mama."

Hansall cringed at the way Will addressed Johanna. He drifted into watching one of the bus' monitors.

Mrs. Coyle had a DVD of *National Treasure* playing, and the opening credits rolled with lush images of DC. Hansall leaned up to talk to Linda.

"Is this supposed to get them to think about history?"

"I think it's supposed to keep them quiet," she said.

"Have you ever watched this movie? It's ridiculous…"

She nodded. "I know."

He moved up to the seat next to her and made himself comfortable. "I don't know what happened to Nicolas Cage."

"Right?" she said. "Remember *Moonstruck*?"

They moved through their favorite Nic Cage movies, surmising that at some point he started doing it for the money. During a lull in the conversation, he held up the glassine envelope with Jobie's cash. "Are you holding money for any of the girls?"

"No," said Linda.

"It's so weird."

"It must be the parents. Have you spoken to them?"

"No. I never met them."

"But, have you *spoken* to them? You know, when Jobie calls home?"

Hansall felt his face burn. "Oh, I've been letting the kids call home on their own."

"Lucky you." She waved toward the girls in the back. "I have to give a full report every night. I haven't been to sleep before midnight."

"Do you know Jobie's parents?"

"Not really." Her voice trailed off. "I saw them once. I've heard they're very nice. I think they do something with computers."

"Is he…what, Japanese? I'm so bad with that, sorry."

"His mom is Vietnamese. His father is German, I think."

"Ah," he said. They both nodded politely, at what he wasn't sure. "I guess they're worried he'll blow the money."

"Guess so."

"I can see why. He wanted to buy a set of spoons for a hundred and thirty bucks."

"A set of *spoons*?" she giggled.

"For his mom. Williamsburg spoons."

"That's so cute."

"Are you kidding?" he said. "She would have killed him and me."

"Oh, I don't know. Any mom would love it a little bit."

"Maybe so," he said. "But Asians and Germans are usually tough with a buck." When he said it, he worried he had gone a bit too far over the boundaries of political correctness. But it was a calculated risk, he thought, the kind white Americans make every day when entering into a new relationship. As he got older, he tested such ground early in conversations, rather than treading lightly for months only to find that the other person — women, really — were bleeding hearts. In his experience, liberal women also tended to be very loud in the morning, and he couldn't deal with loud in the morning.

He was a libertarian, and this leaning got stronger as he aged. He saw government as inept, taxes as legalized theft, and laws as intrusive. Never much of a believer to begin with, he had been a nominal Democrat in college because it helped one get laid, at least at Brown, at least when he was there. His feelings calcified as he matured, and his sense of the meaningless of politics grew the way bread goes stale and then one day is gone.

———

The sun was still in the sky when the Capitol Building appeared on the horizon. The bus left the interstate and pulled into DC. Everything seemed of granite, lending a permanence to its sense of place. That's how it seems to the untrained eye, thought Hansall. He remembered his friends who moved to DC after college speaking only of Happy Hours in Georgetown bars. On the street near an empty manhole cover a white utility van from the phone company or the electric company or the sewer company was parked with "Blazing Hot Internet" advertised on its side.

"Wait, look!" said Mrs. Coyle, jumping up and pointing out the window where the Washington Monument stood like a postcard. "Repeat after me," she yelled to the kids. "Standing at five hundred fifty-five feet and three-quarter inches..." A smattering of voices repeated the phrase back. "C'mon, let me hear you," she said, and then continued, "the world's largest freestanding masonry structure..." She paused: "The Washington Monument." She beamed. The children, catching on now, yelled, "The world's largest freestanding masonry structure...The Washington Monument."

"Every time!" she said. "We say it every time we see it, ok?"

———

The Keybridge Marriott was not much different than the Williamsburg Marriott. To be sure, there were urban touches: the front door was more active, busboys schlepped bags, and people whom Hansall assumed were lobbyists hustled through the lobby. The adults lectured the kids not to wander around unsupervised. When Hansall opened the door to his room, he faced the same forest-green drapes. The minibar situation was no different, signaling to him the power within the chain of policies of bulk-purchasing room finishes. His hopes for airplane bottles of scotch, peanut butter cups, overpriced cashews, Red Bull, and cans of Bud Light were dashed.

He unpacked only his toiletry kit. He could not, would not, face the room and insomnia, lightening darkness, and those drapes—*those drapes*—again. He slapped on aftershave, brushed his teeth, stopped down the hall at the boys' room to make a compulsory plea that they call their mothers, and went to the bar.

It was outfitted in minimalist orange and black tables. The menu featured sushi, steamed dumplings, and Thai salads. The servers were dressed in orange shirts, black slacks, and floral vests. Hansall's mind went again to the decision-making Marriott middle managers. Odds were, every three years they undertook a new theme. "Let's give it a contemporary feel," he heard them say. He saw the budget meetings and the suppressed creativity, perhaps even a maverick within the company pushing for a sushi place. Perhaps the man who spearheaded the innovative restaurant was seen as too big a spender, too ready to go half-cocked into bizarre variations, which served no purpose other than to dilute the brand.

Through his first two scotches Hansall had been watching a plumpish girl two seats away. When she ordered her third vodka and tonic, Hansall said, "Hope you're driving, because I'm not."

She laughed. "Not me, I'm stuck here."

He slid over to the seat next to her. "Me too. Business?"

"Sales trip."

"Don't look so happy about it."

"You have no idea." She crunched her ice. "Day eight."

"Yeah, well, I can beat that."

"Ha. Tell me and tell me slow."

"Field trip." Off her raised eyebrows, he said, "Fifth grade."

"Oh God, kids? From where?"

"California. Santa Monica." She lit up, excited for some reason about Santa Monica.

He ordered two more drinks and the discussion began. He moved like a great running back on a power sweep, sizing up the defense, feinting here and there, applying just enough speed. She was past her window on the looks side, and definitely heavy. This was ok, though — he didn't mind heavy when he was drunk. In his experience, big girls liked to fuck. One drink gave way to three, then five. She put her knee into his thigh and pulled it back. He mentioned his empty room. When he got the right answer, he asked for the check. The tab was one hundred and ten bucks. He decided he didn't want a bar bill on his credit card, for fear it would come up in his deposition, so he reached for cash. All that was left in his wallet was a ten and two ones.

"Do you want me to get it?" said the girl, whose name was Meredith, fishing for her purse. "I ate before you got here."

"That's crazy talk." He found Jobie's glassine envelope and left six twenties on the bar.

———

Hansall came out of a fitful sleep with his left arm was pinned under Meredith's upper body. He saw his face in the mirror from across the room. The air conditioner was on too high, but he didn't want to deal with it, so he stayed beneath the bed's checkered cover and light-yellow sheets. Having rolled over, Meredith's back was to him. He looked at her and was grossed out. He went to his back and stared at the ceiling. His head uncontrollably veered to the right and he saw the drapes. He rolled back toward Meredith, felt the round of her buttocks against him, and felt himself rising. Hansall tried to caress her hair, but it felt like steel wool. He grabbed down along her side and felt her fleshiness. He pushed his hands between her legs, licked his fingers and parted her lips. She groaned and reached back for his head, putting him in a sort of forearm headlock.

They pushed and panted through the sex act for the next fifteen minutes. He grabbed her breasts one at a time from various positions, as though he were reaching down to grab more fruit from a tree. She took on a rubbery resolve, issuing a simple high-pitched grunt each time he thrust. The cold air blowing through the Marriott vents made it impossible to sweat. He buried his head in each available opening of her abundant body, trying to disappear between her legs from the front, between her tits, into her neck, even into her crevices from the side. He put her on her back, on her stomach, put one leg at a time over her head. She complied with each position. He increased the velocity and the force, trying to get her to make more than her basic sound. But nothing worked. He rose onto his forearms and felt his body pound into her until his loud slapping was the only sound he could hear.

He did not know how long he held, but his back started to weaken and he went to his side. He grabbed for her clammy arm and guided her to his crotch. He put a pillow beneath his head and moved her hand faster. She began talking in his ear, and when she saw that he was responding, she spoke more rapidly. She got dirty, then dirtier, then filthy. He put the pillow around his other ear, so that her voice vibrating in his ear louder and louder still was the only thing he could feel. Then he was done. He stared again at the ceiling. Then he turned on his side away from Meredith and looked, once more, at the drapes.

Dark green drifts over him, the color of cold ocean water splashing against a beach, but much grayer, even black. He is in one of those World War II battles from the movies, wearing a green army helmet with netting around it. His unit is mid-invasion, trying to get a foothold amid the shrapnel and flying limbs and smoke and noise. So this is war. It is louder than his imagination allows, and he is in a terror so deep he cannot swallow. He sprints to cover where soil overhangs the beginnings of the shore, with the roots of a long-gone tree fortifying just enough space for a few GIs to find safety. He slams his back into the mound, panting next to two other soldiers. The sound of the bullets is: *pfft*. They are cutting through clothing, piercing into flesh of the men around him.

He is so scared. He sobs. He vows he isn't moving. He looks out to the water where hundreds of other men are swimming back to the boats. The soldier to the right of him clutches his gun and makes signs that he is ready to head back into the fire. He screams in Hansall's ear but his voice is inaudible. Hansall keeps whimpering and looking to the ocean. The solider continues yelling; saliva is pouring out of his mouth. Still Hansall does not budge. The soldier hits Hansall on the helmet, with the butt end of his rifle, screaming all the while, as bullets rattle by. *Pap. C'mon. Pap. Get up. Pap. Get the fuck up. Pap pap. Get up you fucking coward we gotta go. I will leave you here to die in two seconds. Pap, pap, pap.*

Hansall's eyes opened. The noise continued: *pap, pap, pap.* He raised his head. It was someone knocking on the door. Daylight was on the room, a gauzy substance through the sheers. He disentangled from Meredith and groped for his boxer shorts. He stumbled to the door and opened it a crack, pulling the little chain lock taut.

Linda's eyes looked back at him.

"Hey, wanted to make sure you were up…" she said. Before he could react, Linda saw into the secrets of his room. Meredith wrapped herself in a sheet and leisurely went toward the bathroom. Linda's face fell like a stone.

"Ok, wow, I didn't hear the alarm," he said.

Linda backed off the door. "Oh, I'm sorry." She instantaneously recovered. "You overslept. The bus is leaving in five minutes." She held up her wrist to indicate the time. He squinted at her watch as though she must be wrong. Then he glanced back into the room.

"This is not what it looks like. She is an old friend from college — we got drunk and…"

Linda made a none-of-my-business face. "Ok, well, hurry up," and she headed to the elevator. Immediately, a familiar feeling came over him. *Let it all come*, he said to himself. *That's right. I'm a fuckup. I'm an asshole.* The elevator bell rang. He heard Meredith peeing. He closed the door and started packing his day bag.

When he took his seat next to Will, no one was talking. Linda would not meet his eyes, focusing instead on shushing her daughter and then looking out the window.

"Dad, where were you?" said Will. "*Jesus.*"

"Don't talk like that," said Hansall. "Jesus, Will, I got a stomach thing. I was up all night puking."

Mrs. Coyle made the group walk from the Arlington National Cemetery's parking lot to the Tomb of the Unknown Soldier, some two miles uphill. Hansall, head throbbing, trailed closely behind Jobie, who trailed closely behind Will, Declan, and Harry. It had turned cold overnight, and Hansall was suddenly underdressed, cutting the wind in a hooded sweatshirt. He looked at the boys to see if they were wearing enough clothes. The main troika seemed ok, but when he looked at Jobie, something was wrong. Hansall caught up to the boy and felt his shoulder. It was sopping wet.

"Jobie, what happened? You're soaked."

Jobie pushed ahead. "Got splashed on. Ms. Barlow let us swim after dinner and I left my stuff too close to the edge."

"You can't go around like that," said Hansall.

"I'm ok."

Hansall pulled off his own sweatshirt.

"No. Here, take that off and put this on."

Jobie was startled and removed his wet coat. As he took Hansall's sweatshirt, the little boy broke into a wide grin. "This is going to be really big on me," he said. Eventually his bangs poked through the neck and he smiled at Hansall. The sweatshirt was like a gigantic caftan. Hansall helped Jobie push up the sleeves and tucked the back into his jeans as best he could. Jobie looked down at the letters printed across the chest. He looked up at Hansall again. "Brown," he said.

Hansall was not sure what Jobie meant. "Yeah? That's where I went to college. It's called Brown."

"The color brown?"

"Yeah."

Jobie cocked his head in confusion.

"Well, no. It's named after some guy named Brown."

Jobie nodded as though he were a magistrate, or a policeman, or a teacher who had just been presented with a reasonable idea. "Brown," he repeated. Then he ran to catch up with the other boys.

Will drifted next to Hansall a few minutes later, as they passed the picket-fence white headstones, and they walked without speaking. He looked at the boy's straight hair. Will's skin was pale, a bit washed out, especially considering he was a Californian. Hansall wondered, as he often did, what his son's true feelings were toward him. He concluded that it was disappointed love.

Hansall thought of how this contrasted with his own feelings about his parents. He went to memories of his mother rather than his father, probably because she was gone now. Even as a very young boy, he looked forward to being with her. He carried with him images of riding in the Pontiac, the two of them, singing songs on the way to the supermarket. He couldn't wait to get home from school to see her, to hear what she planned to do for the rest of the day. When asked in later life for his earliest memory, he always had the same reply: a Saturday morning play class—a prehistoric Mommy and Me—in which a long, thin foam mat was placed in the middle of the tile floor in the Methodist Church basement, and he and the other kids would practice tumblesaults. He could still see and feel the burnt-red foam, the topside covered with a shiny skin, the bottom spongy and more prone to erosion, little silver-dollar-sized divots probably bitten out by toddlers. He remembered tasting that foam. He remembered his mother's wide-open arms as she motioned for him to tuck his head down and roll toward her.

"Dad," Will said, pointing at a tombstone near the path, "why does that one have just numbers?"

Two rows in, a marble slab did not have a name and life and death details. It read, "11342345."

"It must be a temporary," said Hansall. "Like a placeholder until they get the rest of the info on the soldier." The other boys stopped and looked at it, too.

"No," said Linda, who walked by as they slowed. "That's a serial number. That's what they do when they can't identify the remains."

The long walk uphill ended a few minutes later at the Tomb of the Unknown Soldier. At a whispered command from Mrs. Coyle, they hurried to catch the Changing of the Guard. Right on the hour, the children stretched on their tiptoes to see the clicking and clacking soldiers march back and forth along the marble, until the retiring sentry was replaced by the new man, who took his place in the guard box, face chiseled into a glare. As Hansall took in the new marine's final position, sideways, he wondered if the guards were really guarding anything.

The group made their way from the monument.

"So no one knows who he is?" said Will.

"Nope," Hansall said.

"Not even his family?" said Declan.

"Not even the army people?" said Harry.

"Someone must have known when they buried him," said Will.

"They told them to forget," said Jobie. "They told anybody that knew about him to forget him. His mother, his brother, sister."

"That's crazy," said Harry.

"War is hell," said Jobie with a shrug.

———

When they reached the Visitor's Center on their way to the bus, the kids swarmed into yet another gift shop. Hansall marveled at the consistency of the color scheme. It, too, was beige, with new carpet and brown shelves. The workers again wore vague uniforms, and the kids scattered among the souvenirs. He stood at the entranceway, near the checkout counter, near but not talking to a cluster of teachers and moms.

Jobie approached him. "Can I have my money?"

"What is it this time?"

He held up a glossy coffee-table book. "I need fifty-five." Hansall noticed Mrs. Coyle heading over, and, figuring he had backup, looked sternly at the kid.

"C'mon, Jobie," he said, loud enough for the teacher to hear. "Not again. You can't spend that kind of money."

"What's he saying?" Mrs. Coyle said.

"We're at it again," Hansall explained, rolling his eyes. "He wants fifty-five bucks to buy a book."

Jobie held up the book. *The Illustrated History of the Tomb of the Unknown Soldier.* He glared at Hansall, then turned to Mrs. Coyle. "It's my money."

Hansall took the book out of his hand. "Jobie, we said n—"

"Well," Mrs. Coyle interrupted. "I don't think that's so bad. Is this what you really want?"

Jobie nodded. She looked at Hansall and turned her palms and said, "Let him get it. It's a nice book."

Jobie snatched the book back from Hansall and got in the checkout line. Hansall shuffled to the line and stood without speaking to Jobie, watching the checkers slide items into the clear plastic gift bags. Hansall thought, *This is a cemetery, for crissakes.*

Then a bolt of panic hit him as reached in his pocket. He didn't have Jobie's money. Hansall knew he could not pull out a credit card, because the kid would freak out if he didn't see the money come from his envelope. Hansall scoured the inside of the shop for an ATM but couldn't find a machine. The checker said, "Next."

"Hi," Hansall said in his nicest voice. The checker was yet another retiree, a rail-thin man with a gray beard. "Hey, can I give you a check?"

The man shook his head. "No checks." Hansall glanced down and saw Jobie leaning in. Hansall snuck a look at what money he had left in his pants pocket. Sixteen dollars. Behind him, the line of tourists waiting to throw down for Arlington National Cemetery swag was backing up. The old man behind the register stared at him. Then he shifted his gaze to Hansall's right.

Linda was at his side. "How much is it?" she said. She ignored Hansall and handed the checker three twenties. She retrieved her change and the book, now encased in a large clear gift bag, and handed it to Jobie. She put her hand on the small of the boy's back and guided him out of the store.

They shuttled their way through the rest of the day. A blindingly fast trip to the Air and Space Museum at the Smithsonian left the boys unsatisfied, and Hansall toyed with the idea of inciting a gender fight on behalf of his guys. Where they wanted to linger with astronaut uniforms and retrorockets, the women running the show hurried them back onto the bus. But the group dynamic reclaimed even Hansall when they passed the Washington Monument, and by now the kids did not have to wait for Mrs. Coyle to start the chant. Jobie, in fact, seemed on perpetual lookout, and he jumped up and shouted, "Standing at five hundred fifty-five feet and three-quarter inches..."

The rest of the bus joined in, "The world's largest freestanding masonry structure..." Hansall found himself catching on to the cadence, chiming in with the others, swept up by the natural force of ringing in on something. He looked down at Will, who was beaming as he gave full-throated voice with the other kids, proud as they were of accomplishment in memorizing the words, in memorializing the Memorial. He smiled at his dad.

"...The Washington Monument."

———

Hansall's brief bubble of belonging was burst at the National Archive, where the Websters stood in line outside of the building for forty-five minutes. As they waited, the women seemed to enclose around Linda. Rather than hanging back and bridging the gender gap as she had been doing throughout the trip, a shuttle diplomat of sorts, determined to keep the peace and find common ground with Hansall, she was returning to her female nation-state. The mothers and teachers surrounded her, their arms touched her, they practically hugged her. Their private laughter rang at him, a stuck-out tongue.

The boys were ensconced in a ridiculous conversation about bonus patches for *Grand Theft Auto*, so, as they moved into the somber old building, Hansall felt, once again, alone. The big news at the National Archive was not even national. The Magna Carta was on temporary loan from wherever it was housed, or, more accurately, wherever it was that housed the earliest copies of the Magna Carta, of which there were apparently only five, that being the number of Magna Cartas that were needed to proclaim the new normal across England in 1215. It was unclear to Hansall which Magna Carta was in front of them now, but it was plain that any one of the early copies was so special that it warranted first-stop special-guest-star status on the United States National Archive tour of Freedom's

Greatest Hits. Hansall wondered if it shouldn't read "3/5" at the lower right-hand corner, like a very limited and very valuable Warhol lithograph.

The light around the glass-encased parchment made clear viewing impossible. He had a recollection of a World War II novel in which a bunch of German soldiers went through an elaborate plan to kill Winston Churchill, only to find out that the man they ultimately took out was not Winston Churchill but an impostor used by the British to fake everyone out. Instincts ignited, Hansall found it suspect that the English would let the U.S. have *any* of the real Magna Cartas. The kids peered in at the grand old document, their faces hopeful but vacant. They hadn't yet covered the Magna Carta in social studies, Ms. Barlow explained. Hansall wondered what the hell the children could possibly be grasping from this. What was a kid growing up three thousand miles away going to get out of fifteen seconds in front of this abstract reduction? All anyone ever understood about the Magna Carta was that it was the granddaddy of them all, like the Rose Bowl.

Onward through the Archive they zoomed, taking in the Declaration of Independence, The Constitution, and The Emancipation Proclamation, collectively, in less time than they spent waiting to use the urinals at lunchtime on the scalding day in Williamsburg. Hansall brought Will back for a second look at the Bill of Rights, dutifully trying to attach significance to the one thing on this journey he wanted his son to understand.

"All of our freedom — everything — comes from this paragraph, if you ask me," he said, pointing to the First

Amendment. To their credit, the boys, including Jobie, went to their tiptoes.

Will pointed to a place lower on the piece of parchment. "Dad, what is the Seventh Amendment?"

Hansall felt the wave of panic he always felt when he should know something but did not. He was a fake. He had faked everything—high school, college, law school. He knew there were objective measures such as diplomas and the bar exam, but felt nonetheless that if he were the real deal, he would remember the Seventh Amendment.

"It's complicated," he said, in an authoritative voice. "It has to do with states' rights...the rights of the states."

"Really?" said Declan.

"Of course," said Jobie. "Mr. Hansall is a lawyer. That's what lawyers study, the Constitution and the amendments."

———

Hansall's hangover did not improve during the long, hot day, and by the time they finished a hectic dinner in Chinatown, he was exhausted. Next the group took on the Korean Memorial, with its statues of soldiers moving through rice paddies. The GIs had green pit helmets, with the netting and packs of cigarettes fastened in the band. The memorial was made up of a wall of superimposed images, snapshots of young men at war, portraits taken by Polaroid during down times. Mrs. Coyle told the kids to look closely for a dog, and at the end of the wall collage, one of the girls jumped and squealed and pointed to a German shepherd in the arms of two infantrymen.

Will and Hansall stared at the picture. Hansall noticed the boy was upset.

"It makes me think of Rusty," Will said.

Hansall and Johanna had purchased Rusty as a puppy in happier times, and he had become Will's dog. Rusty had to be put down several months earlier, on New Year's Eve. Hansall had not come to the house for the vet's visit, at the conclusion of which it was decided Rusty had suffered long enough. Johanna told Hansall the next day, while he was watching the Rose Bowl.

"Well, buddy, Rusty is in a better place now." Seeing that didn't work very well, Hansall nodded to the picture. "Just like that guy. He's long gone by now, too."

Will rushed ahead to find Declan. Per Mrs. Coyle's instruction, the children held hands as they moved through the mass of spring breakers splaying out over the conjunction of memorials surrounding the mall and made their way to the steps of the Lincoln. Swept up in goal gradient and overtired, they ran up the white granite stairs, and Hansall struggled to keep up. When he arrived at the top, the group had turned and was looking out. It was just becoming dark, and the Washington Monument stood at the end of the reflecting pool, with the Capitol Building on the horizon.

"You all remember Martin Luther King, whom we talked about," said Ms. Coyle. "Well, you are standing right where he stood when he gave the speech. Who can remember what the speech was called?"

Hands shot up and several of the kids strained to get her attention. "Let's see how much the parents know," she said. "Who can answer? Linda?"

"It was the *I Have a Dream* speech."

"That's right."

"It's also the spot where protesters about UFOs come to give speeches," said Hansall. He laughed and looked around to the other adults with a smile.

"Let's go in and look at Lincoln's statue," said Mrs. Coyle.

Hansall's ears burned. The chilly air of polite dislike seemed to be giving way to quiet whispers that maybe something needed to be done with him. Well, they were all too serious, he thought. He didn't care to buy into treating this all like the classroom. The boys were looking for distraction, something to break up the monotony.

He had an idea based on a memory from his high school trip years ago. He steered his foursome to the side of the memorial, where excerpts of Lincoln's two inaugural addresses were written in huge block letters.

"Look up there" he said. "There is a mistake in one of those columns. Which one of you can find it first?"

Hansall gave them hints, directing them to the far left, then to the lower half, and finally, when it did not appear that they were going to get it, he directed them to the place in the sixth sentence of the second paragraph of the first inaugural address where the E in the word *Earth* was actually an F. It took another minute for the boys to see exactly where he was pointing, but eventually they all found the flaw and smiled. Each of them looked at him with brimming satisfaction, excited to have caught the memorial makers in a mistake.

Mrs. Coyle was commandeering the group to the other side of the building. A soft din was over the place, the congealed sound of hundreds of school kids milling, the echoes and guide voices bouncing off the grand stone and slate of the compound.

"Ok," she said. "I do this with every class I bring here. Look on the wall. We are going to read it out loud together. Parents too. Ok, ready? Everyone scooch in close. Jobie, start us off."

Jobie gazed up at the letters.

"*Four score...*"

The rest of the kids' voices came in, "*And seven years ago...*"

Hansall smirked. He looked down to try the boys' eyes, to see if they were buying it. But when Linda shot him one of her sideways looks, like his mother, midprayer at church, and he saw that the boys all had their heads forward, he merged in. "*Now we are engaged in a great Civil War, testing whether that nation, or any nation so conceived and so dedicated, can long endure.*"

Well, he thought, it *was* a damn good speech. He focused on the sound of the words. The kids' voices made a sort of chamber music. As they mouthed the lines, they closed in tighter: "*As a final resting place for those who gave their lives here so that that nation might live.*"

The words, the curious diction, came back to him. He remembered staying up late one night in his room during high school, reading the speech from his history book and trying to memorize the lines. He had opened and closed the book for hours, repeating the phrases out loud until he had the whole thing. The mnemonic tools he used came back to him: three paragraphs, one sentence in the first paragraph, three sentences in the second. He gave into just reading along with the young voices. "*The world will little note or long remember what we say here, but it will not forget what they did here.*"

What a great line. *"It will not forget what they did here..."* The writing was perfect in every way. He looked at the children's faces. They were in T-shirts and laceless sneakers, the boys with long hair and the girls skinny and tallish. *"It is rather for us to be here dedicated to the great task remaining before us—that from these honored dead we take increased devotion to that cause for which they gave the last full measure of devotion..."*

As he said "that from these honored dead," Hansall felt a hitch in his throat. His eyes began to water. Mrs. Coyle looked at him and seemed to give him an infinitesimal nod. He heard his voice in the voice of the kids. *"That this nation, under God, shall have a new birth of freedom—and that government of the people, by the people, for the people, shall not perish from the earth."*

———

The next day, their last, a road warrior feeling held the tables where the Webster parents and kids ate their scrambled eggs sleepy-eyed, but now accustomed to it, like soldiers at mess. Their suitcases were ready, their sleeping bags were rolled tight.

As the bus pulled onto the freeway on the road to Mount Vernon, the last stop of the week, Hansall studied Will leaning against the window next to him; he was watching the road.

"Hey, man, how are you doing?" Hansall said.

"Fine."

"It's been a good trip. Don't you think it's been a good trip? We've had fun, haven't we?"

"Yeah, Dad. Sure."

The kid never really gave him a chance. He never let down his guard, his loyalty to his mother never left the dynamic. Women weren't above involving the kids—to Hansall, that was one of the biggest jokes going. He kept looking at Will, hoping they could seize in this moment a little connection.

"Dad, why'd you do it?" Will said finally.

"Why did I do what?"

"You know."

"No, Will, I don't know. Why did I do what? What has your mother told you that I did?"

"Forget it," Will said and pushed past him and headed for the back of the bus. Hansall stared forward. Mrs. Coyle had put a DVD about the preparations the soldiers go through for the changing of the guard ceremony. It was called *Honor at Arlington*.

———

Mount Vernon, he knew, was a poor second to Monticello, and the bus wasn't far out of DC proper when he realized that the cacophonous mother who claimed at breakfast they were headed to Jefferson's home had been wrong. He wrote it off to exhaustion that he didn't catch the mistake at first blush; of course they wouldn't drive all the way down to Charlottesville, which would have taken hours. Fitting that they would end with Washington, Hansall thought. First in War, Peace, and the Minds of his Countrymen, and the last stop on the way back to California.

Dignified signs announced Mount Vernon's proximity, and a massive parking maze oozing of public/ private cooperative fundraising dumped them into a horseshoe-curved unloading zone. From there they were funneled toward the main house and quickly joined the line on one side of the long circular driveway leading to the old building.

As a schoolteacher in front of them rattled on about Washington's love of trees, Hansall deduced from a sign under the nearby walnut that there was a fifty-five-minute wait from their current spot. They inched up the white pebble pathway, moving just often enough to distinguish what they were doing from standing. Mrs. Coyle sensed she was losing everyone, so she reached into her pocketbook and produced a colonial trivia book collection.

"Which political party did George Washington belong to?"

"Republicans," said one kid.

"Nope."

"Democrats," said another.

"Uh-uh. Republicans and Democrats didn't exist back then."

With that, the kids were out of ideas. The group inched in the line but kept looking at the teacher.

"Parents?" Mrs. Coyle said..

After a moment, a ginger-haired mother said, "Federalists?" She said it as though she was speaking for the group, like the appointed family leader on *Family Feud*. Her eyes petitioned the other moms for support.

"Nope."

"Then the Antifederalists?" ginger-mom said, laughing at her own cleverness. The moms grinned and avoided eye contact with Mrs. Coyle.

"No party," said Hansall, from the side. He said it without thinking, reflexively. "He was above party."

"That's right," said Mrs. Coyle. She put her hands on Jobie's shoulders, and pointed him up the path, as they moved with the mass of people another few steps toward the mansion.

Inside, the place seemed to Hansall incredibly small. All the more so when the docent said, "In one calendar year, 1783, after he was back from the war, Washington and Martha had six hundred and forty-two houseguests."

Hansall said to an eavesdropping old lady in the group behind them, "Jeez, I don't even like it when my sister wants to bring her kids out for spring break."

Once finished with the inside, the guide concluded the tour on the back porch overlooking a broad lawn with a beautiful view of the Potomac. "No matter where he went — and he went everywhere his country asked, because he never refused a request for service — General Washington always, *always* longed for nothing more than to be back in this spot. Yet he hardly ever was able to get here."

After the speech the group was free to roam. Hansall watched as Will and Declan and Harry ran down toward the river's edge. He noticed Jobie walking with one of the girls, deep in discussion. It *was* a beautiful view, Hansall noted for himself. The tourists were diffusing over the lawn. He saw Linda taking in the horizon as well. He moved her way.

"Beautiful," he said. "I feel like I've been here longer than George himself."

She nodded but didn't laugh. They both kept looking forward.

"I know how he felt," Hansall said. When Linda looked at him, he continued, "You know...he just wanted to be left alone."

She took that in with another nod and kept looking at the river. After a moment, she turned and stared at him.

"Really? Really, Doug?" She was suddenly livid. Like she was over something, past it. "You really know how George Washington felt?"

Taken by surprise, he became quiet. "It's a joke," he said.

She made a scoffing noise. "You're a real piece of shit, you know that?" She was gone by the time he tried to respond.

———

Mrs. Coyle had allotted a mind-bending six hours for the visit to Mount Vernon. She figured they could take the day exploring its grounds, gardens, and underground museum before heading for the plane. The specter had, for Hansall, the punishing feeling of the day at Williamsburg, on a somewhat smaller scale, like a reprise of a boring song in the second act of a bad musical. The Websters ground their way through the servant's quarters, the blacksmith shed, and the scullery. They spent an hour trudging through the private cemetery, culminating with a solemn procession past the minimausoleum containing the great man's cement tomb. Martha's coffin was next to George's, albeit much smaller — Hansall was gobsmacked to learn she was five foot one. He had always thought of her as a broad woman, with childbearing hips and lots of flesh — the only one who held George under her thumb.

He pondered this as he sat on a bench on the bottom floor of the museum building waiting for the day to end. He was in the Ye Olde Refreshment Center, a hybrid cafeteria and fast-food restaurant. On one side, cashiers with three-cornered hats took the money of guests who ordered burgers and fries from short-order cooks and slid their trays down aluminum counters, past self-serve soda fountains dispensing Styrofoam cupfuls of Pepsi, Sprite, and Mr. Pibb. On the other side of the pavilion, a shopping-mall-styled McDonald's coexisted, a marvel of cooperation, he thought, between local and national food service.

He had long since lost track of the boys, or anyone from the group. To pass the time he ate. Reasoning that locals produced better food, he hit the Mount Vernon side for an order of fried chicken and macaroni and cheese. He washed it down with a thirty-two-ounce Diet Pepsi and a white-chocolate-chip and macadamia nut cookie.

———

When the bus pulled into the unloading zone at Dulles Airport—yet another horseshoe curve—the headlights of the scores of vehicles jockeying for position cut into the night. The driver didn't turn the engines off, and as the kids piled off and were directed to pick up their bags by the chaperones, Hansall had to yell at Miss Barlow to be heard.

"I have to take off," he said, jerking his thumb over his shoulder. "Will knows. I have a different ticket—had to do it because I came through New York. I will catch up with you guys at the gate." With that he found Will and gave him a touch on the shoulder and a wave. He mouthed, "I'll get it taken care of, and I will see you guys in a few minutes."

He breezed up to the check-in counter, used the electronic kiosk, and was off to the Elite Gold Service security gate. As it happened, each of the lines to the nine metal detectors was empty, and he was through in no time. He checked the monitor and found it was 6:48. He had a full half hour to himself before having to get to the gate with the kids for the eight-thirty takeoff.

To his surprise, there was a decent-looking sushi bar on his way to the D terminal. Within ten minutes he had downed a Kirin Light and asked for another. An order of yellowtail sushi and a spicy tuna roll appeared. Men in suits and stylish women spoke in non-airport ways to the bartenders. It was a rare high-end airport spot with well-dressed regulars, business travelers shuttling to New York and Chicago.

He relaxed and shot the breeze with the waitress until seven thirty. He found an ATM and placed money into Jobie's envelope, subtracting a credible amount for meals and the glossy book from Arlington. On the upswing now for sure, he imagined a smooth accounting to Jobie's parents at the pick-up in LA. Buzzed up by the beer and sake, he glided toward the gate at 7:35. But, when he made it to Gate D-9, the group from Santa Monica was nowhere to be found. He double checked the destination listed on the sign. Yes, the flight at Gate D-9 was to LA, and it was on time. He realized that in his reverie of the liberty of the last hour since he left the group he had not checked his phone. He looked down to find three messages from a number he didn't recognize. He punched into his voicemail.

"Hi, Doug? It's Dana Barlow. You just left and we're here with the kids at the security gate. They won't let us through because you're not here. They say you are part of our economy ticket allotment and they can't put us through till we're all here. If you get this, please call me."

It didn't come as a complete surprise. He knew his assistant was having trouble rebooking the ticket, and now he remembered he had said, "Just get me my own ticket in First Class." He listened to the other two messages. The last was from 7:20 and Dana was clearly starting to worry the group would miss the plane. Hansall began to dial the number, but he stopped. There were no unoccupied seats in the waiting area. He headed to an empty floor space near an electrical outlet. He found his charger and plugged in his phone.

At 7:45, he saw Linda's daughter and several other girls coming down the terminal corridor. Then the others, like so many wagon trains drifting along. Mrs. Coyle walked alongside Will, Jobie, Declan, and Harry. Hansall ran toward them.

"What happened? Where were you guys?" Hansall asked, pretending to be worried.

Mrs. Coyle said, "Dana tried to call you, didn't you get the message?"

He pointed at his phone in the wall. "Oh man, I've been out of juice." He opened his hands, asking for an explanation.

"They wouldn't let us in without you," said Mrs. Coyle. "Some security thing. Did you not get rid of your other ticket?"

"They wouldn't let me buy a coach ticket…" he lied. "That was the problem. That's why I had to go in first."

By then, the whole group had walked past and was on to the gate area. Hansall said to Mrs. Coyle, "Well, at least we made it," and headed for the boys, who sat on the floor and pulled out their phones.

Jobie went to Mrs. Coyle and tugged her arm. In turn, she looked at Hansall. "Doug," she said, "will you take him to the bathroom?"

"Sure. C'mon, Jobie."

As he walked Jobie toward the men's room, Hansall said, "Did you have a fun trip?"

"Oh, yes," Jobie said. He was calmer than he had been before. Hansall wondered if it was from exhaustion. When they started back to the gate, Jobie spied a concession stand. "Mr. Hansall," he said, "can I get a Coke?"

"Sure," said Hansall. They waited in line without saying anything, the little boy standing next to him. When the cashier handed Hansall the soda, Jobie started to dig in his pockets to pay. Hansall said, "I got it, man. Remember? I've had all your money. Put your change away."

"Oh." Jobie seemed genuinely touched. "Thank you." He clicked open the Coke can and drank lustily as they started back to the gate. It struck Hansall that Jobie's had gained an air of confidence that had not been present before. Jobie wasn't nervous, or preoccupied with not getting lost, and instead surveyed the comings and goings of the airport like a scientist looking for patterns. Just as they were returning to the group, he looked up resolutely and said, "Mr. Hansall?"

"Yes?"

"Thank you for being my parent chaperone."

"Hey, no problem," Hansall said. "No problem at all. Thanks for being such a good boy."

The gate attendant announced boarding for first class and any uniformed military service people. "Ok, guys," Hansall said to the boys, who were gathered by a wall outlet, watching Declan play FIFA World Cup. He motioned to the boarding area. "I have to get on now— they're making me get on. Be good on the plane, I will come back to check on you after we get in the air."

He headed down the Jetway. When he arrived at 3A, he removed his iPad and a plastic pill bottle preloaded with Xanax and Ambien from his bag. A male flight attendant came to him with a tray of orange juice and champagne.

Hansall was just settling into a profile of a billionaire hedge-fund manager who was now revitalizing the Salvation Army when he noticed that the gate attendant, a natty man with a blue V-neck sweater over his shirt and tie, had boarded the plane and was talking with one of the female flight attendants. They looked at a computer printout and then approached Hansall.

"Excuse me, Mr. Hansall?" said the man.

"Yup."

"May I see your boarding pass?"

"And your reservation number or any other paperwork you have," said the stewardess.

Hansall stood and retrieved his bag from the overhead department. He handed them his boarding pass. "I don't really have anything else." While they conferred over the boarding pass, Hansall said, "I think I know what this is about. I may be double booked. My assistant had to route me through New York, and I got a separate ticket from the group I'm with…"

"Right, the school group," the gate attendant said, and looked at the woman. "He must also have a seat in first."

"Is there a problem?" Hansall said.

A line of passengers was stacking up behind them trying to board the plane, so the pair stepped into the row in front of Hansall and leaned over the seats to continue speaking to him.

"Well," said the man, "we have someone under your name in two separate seats. That sets off all kinds of bells." The line of passengers flowed past them toward the economy section. "The security system gets fouled up when someone takes two seats."

"Hi, Dad," said Will, making his way past Hansall to his seat, with Declan, Harry, and Jobie in tow.

"Oh, hey man," said Hansall. "Go along back there to your seat, don't hold people up."

"Are you in trouble or something?"

"No, no. Just get going." Hansall turned back to his interrogators. "My son," he explained. "I'm with his school group."

"I know," said the woman. The kids and mothers were all walking by now. Ms. Barlow passed him and lifted her eyebrows. Linda ignored him.

After another moment looking at the printouts, the gate attendant seemed to have an idea. "Mr. Hansall, do you want to sit in the back with your group? We have several requests for upgrades…That could make it easy."

"No, of course not," Hansall shot back. There was an awkward moment before Hansall said, "Don't you have standbys? Just give the other seat to someone going standby."

They shook their heads. "Not that easy," said the woman. They continued to stare at the printouts, until the man finally said to the flight attendant, "Well, it's up to the captain. It's his call."

After ten minutes, the plane was fully boarded, but the door had not been closed. Hansall said yes to another glass of champagne and downed it. The man in the v-neck lingered on, making small talk with the two flight attendants.

The door to the cockpit opened and the captain emerged, bending his head to get through the door, and then uncoiling to his full height. Peeking from his seat, it looked to Hansall like he was six three or six four. He listened as the gate attendant showed him the printout. Eventually Hansall heard the captain say, "Where is he? Show me." The female attendant pointed to Hansall, who stared down at his *New Yorker* but was able to peek back up and see the captain mumble something to the other three workers before ducking back into the cockpit.

And then miraculously the door of the plane was shut and Hansall was relieved of his worries. Takeoff announcements were made. The male flight attendant made one last pass through the cabin, taking glasses and making sure cell phones were turned off. As he reached down to take the champagne glass, Hansall said, "What did the captain say about my situation?"

The flight attendant leaned down to whisper in Hansall's ear. "He said it was up to you."